Edgar Wallace was born illegitim[illegible] adopted by George Freeman, a port[illegible] eleven, Wallace sold newspapers at [illegible] school took a job with a printer. He enlisted in the Royal West Kent Regiment, later transferring to the Medical Staff Corps and was sent to South Africa. In 1898 he published a collection of poems called *The Mission that Failed*, left the army and became a correspondent for Reuters.

Wallace became the South African war correspondent for *The Daily Mail*. His articles were later published as *Unofficial Dispatches* and his outspokenness infuriated Kitchener, who banned him as a war correspondent until the First World War. He edited the *Rand Daily Mail*, but gambled disastrously on the South African Stock Market, returning to England to report on crimes and hanging trials. He became editor of *The Evening News*, then in 1905 founded the Tallis Press, publishing *Smith*, a collection of soldier stories, and *Four Just Men*. At various times he worked on *The Standard*, *The Star*, *The Week-End Racing Supplement* and *The Story Journal*.

In 1917 he became a Special Constable at Lincoln's Inn and also a special interrogator for the War Office. His first marriage to Ivy Caldecott, daughter of a missionary, had ended in divorce and he married his much younger secretary, Violet King.

The Daily Mail sent Wallace to investigate atrocities in the Belgian Congo, a trip that provided material for his *Sanders of the River* books. In 1923 he became Chairman of the Press Club and in 1931 stood as a Liberal candidate at Blackpool. On being offered a scriptwriting contract at RKO, Wallace went to Hollywood. He died in 1932, on his way to work on the screenplay for *King Kong*.

BY THE SAME AUTHOR
ALL PUBLISHED BY HOUSE OF STRATUS

Big Foot
The Black Abbot
Bones In London
Bones of the River
The Clue of the Twisted Candle
The Daffodil Mystery
The Frightened Lady
The Joker
Sanders
The Square Emerald
The Three Just Men
The Three Oak Mystery

Mr Justice Maxell

This edition published in 2001 by House of Stratus, an imprint of Stratus Holdings plc, 24c Old Burlington Street, London, W1X 1RL, UK.

www.houseofstratus.com

Typeset, printed and bound by House of Stratus.

A catalogue record for this book is available from the British Library.

ISBN 1-84232-701-1

1

It was two hours after the muezzin had called to evening prayer, and night had canopied Tangier with a million stars. In the little Sok, the bread-sellers sat cross-legged behind their wares, their candles burning steadily, for there was not so much as the whisper of a wind blowing. The monotonous strumming of a guitar from a Moorish café, the agonised *barlak!* of a belated donkey-driver bringing his charge down the steep streets which lead to the big bazaar, the shuffle of bare feet on Tangier's cobbles, and the distant hush-hush of the rollers breaking upon the amber shore – these were the only sounds which the night held.

John Maxell sat outside the Continental Café, in the condition of bodily content which a good dinner induces. Mental content should have accompanied such a condition, but even the memory of a perfect dinner could not wholly obliterate a certain uneasiness of mind. He had been uneasy when he came to Tangier, and his journey through France and Spain had been accompanied by certain apprehensions and doubts which Cartwright had by no means dispelled.

Rather, by his jovial evasions, his cheery optimism, and at times his little irritable outbreaks of temper, he had given the eminent King's Counsel further cause for disquiet.

Cartwright sat at the other side of the table, and was unusually quiet. This was a circumstance which was by no means displeasing to Maxell, for the night was not conducive to talk. There are in Northern Africa many nights like this, when one wishes to sit in dead silence and let thought take its own course, unchecked and untrammelled. In

Morocco such nights are common and, anyway, Maxell had always found it difficult to discuss business matters after dinner.

Cartwright had no temperament and his quiet was due to other causes. It was he who broke the silence, knocking out his pipe on the iron-topped table with a clang which jarred his more sensitive companion to the very spine.

"I'd stake my life and my soul on there being a reef," he said with a suddenness which was almost as jarring. "Why, you've seen the outcrop for yourself, and isn't it exactly the same formation as you see on the Rand?"

Maxell nodded.

Though a common-law man, he had been associated in mining cases and had made a very careful study of the whole problem of gold extraction.

"It looks right enough to me," he said, "but as against that we have the fact that some clever engineers have spent a great deal of time and money trying to locate the reef. That there is gold in Morocco everybody knows, and I should say, Cartwright, that you are right. But where is the reef? It would cost a fortune to bore, even though we had the other borings to guide us."

The other made an impatient noise.

"Of course, if the reef were all mapped out it would be a simple matter, but then we shouldn't get on to it, as we are today, at the cost of a few thousands. Hang it all, Maxell, we've got to take a certain amount of risk! I know it's a gamble quite as well as you. There's no sense in arguing that point with me. But other things are gambles too. Law was a gamble to you for many years, and a bigger gamble after you took silk."

This was a sore point with Maxell, as the other knew. A prosperous junior, he had been called within the Bar, and taken upon himself the function and style of King's Counsellor in the hope that his prosperity would still further be expanded. And, like so many other men, he had discovered that the successful junior is not necessarily the successful KC.

Fortunately for him, he had long before contested and won a seat in Parliament, and his service to the Government of the day had to some extent ensured his future. But, financially, he had suffered considerably.

"No," he said, "silk isn't any great catch to a man, I agree; and it was certainly a gamble, and a losing gamble."

"Which reminds me," said Cartwright, "there was a talk, before I left London, that you would be given Cabinet rank."

Maxell laughed.

"It is extremely unlikely," he said. "Anyway, if they make me Solicitor-General, that doesn't carry Cabinet rank."

"It carries a lot of money," said Cartwright after a pause for a moment, "and it's money that counts just now, Maxell."

Again the lawyer nodded.

He might have added that, but for the need for money, he would long since have dropped his association with Alfred Cartwright, though Cartwright's name stood very high in certain circles of the City of London. They had been at school together, though in that period there had been no very great friendship between them. And Cartwright was marked out for success from the beginning. He inherited a considerable business when his father died, and he enlarged and improved upon it. He had taken up a hundred and one outside interests, and had made most of them pay. A few of them did not pay, and it was whispered that the losses upon his failures took a considerable slice of the balance that accrued from his successes.

They had met again when Maxell was a junior and Cartwright the defendant in a case which, had he lost, would have made him some thirty thousand pounds the poorer. When Maxell thought back upon that event, he had to confess that it was not a pleasant case, being one in which Cartwright had been charged with something which was tantamount to misrepresentation; and, although he had won, and won brilliantly, he had never felt any great pride in his achievement.

"No," he said (the pauses were frequent and long), "I should hardly imagine that the Prime Minister loves me to that extent. In Parliament you have to be an uncomfortable quantity to be really successful. You must be strong enough to have a national following, and sufficiently independent to keep the Whips guessing. I am known as a safe man, and I hold a safe seat, which I couldn't lose if I tried. That doesn't make for promotion. Of course, I could have had an Under-Secretaryship for the asking, and that means a couple of thousand a year, but it also means that you last out the life of the administration in a subordinate capacity, and that, by the time you have made good, your party is in the cold shade of opposition, and there are no jobs going."

He shook his head, and returned immediately to the question of the missing reef, as though he wished to take the subject from his own personal affairs.

"You say that it would cost us a lot of money if the reef was proved," he said. "Isn't it costing us a lot now?"

Cartwright hesitated.

"Yes, it is. As a matter of fact," he confessed, "the actual reef is costing nothing, or next to nothing, because El Mograb is helping me. In our own business – that is to say, in the Syndicate – our expenses are more or less small; but I am doing a little independent buying, and that has meant the spending of money. I am taking up all the ground to the south of the Angera – a pretty expensive business."

Maxell shifted uneasily in his chair.

"That is rather worrying me, you know, Cartwright," he said; "your scheme is ever so much too ambitious. I was figuring it out this afternoon as I was sitting in my room, and I came to the conclusion that, if the scheme as you outlined it to me yesterday went through, it would mean your finding two millions."

"Three," corrected the other cheerfully, "but think what it means, Maxell! Supposing it went through. Supposing we struck a reef, and the reef continued, as I believe it will, through the country I am taking up! Why, it may mean a hundred millions to me!"

The other sighed.

"I have reached the point where I think a hundred thousand is an enormous sum," he said. "However, you know your own business best, Cartwright. But I want to be satisfied in the matter in which we are associated together, that my liability does not exceed my power to pay. And there is another matter."

Cartwright guessed the "other matter."

"Well?" he asked.

"I was looking over your titles this afternoon," said Maxell, "and I see no reference to the old Spanish working. I remember that you told me a Spaniard had taken up a considerable stretch of country and had exhausted his capital trying to prove the reef – Señor Brigot, wasn't that his name?"

The other nodded curtly.

"A drunkard – and a bad lot," he said. "He's broke."

Maxell smiled.

"His moral character doesn't count so far as the details go; what does matter is that if your theory is correct, the reef must run through his property. What are you going to do about that?"

"Buy him out," said the other.

He rose abruptly.

"I'm walking up to the Sok," he said. "Come along?"

They tramped up the long, steep hill-street together, and they did not speak till they had passed through the ancient gate into the unrelieved gloom which lies outside the city.

"I don't understand you, Maxell – you take an old man's view of things," said Cartwright irritably. "You're comparatively young, you're a good-looker. Why the devil don't you marry, and marry money?"

Maxell laughed.

"Have you ever tried to marry money?" he asked dryly.

"No," said the other after a pause, "but I should think it is pretty simple."

"Try it," said the laconic Maxell. "It is simple in books, but in real life it is next to impossible. I go about a great deal in society of all kinds, and I can tell you that I have never yet met an eligible spinster with money – that is to say, large money. I agree with you," he went on after a while, "a man like myself should marry. And he should marry well. I could give a woman a good position, but she's got to be the right kind of woman. There are some times when I'm just frantic about my position. I am getting older – I am forty-seven next birthday – and every day that slips past is a day lost. I ought to be married, but I can't afford a wife. It is a blackguardly thing to talk about money in connection with marriage and yet somehow I can think of nothing else – whenever the thought arises in my mind I see an imaginary beauty sitting on a big bag of gold!" He chuckled to himself. "Let's go back," he said, "the big Sok always gives me the creeps."

Something lumbered past him in the darkness, some big, overpowering beast with an unpleasant smell, and a guttural voice cried in Arabic: "Beware!"

"Camels!" said Cartwright briefly. "They're bringing in the stuff for the morning market. The night's young yet, Maxell. Let us go up to the theatre."

"The theatre?" said Maxell. "I didn't even know the theatre was open."

"It is called theatre by courtesy," explained Cartwright; "the inhabitants refer to it as the circus. It's a big wooden place on the sea edge – "

"I know it, I know it," said Maxell. "What is being played? The only people I have ever seen there have been Spanish artistes – and pretty bad artistes, too."

"Well, there's a treat for you. It is an English company, or rather, a variety company with a number of English turns," said Cartwright. "We might do worse – at least, I might," he added ominously.

When they reached the theatre they found it sparsely filled. Cartwright took one of the open boxes, and his companion settled himself into a corner to smoke. The turns were of the kind which are usually to be met with on the Levant; a tawdrily attired lady sang a humorous song in Spanish, the humour being frankly indecent. There were a juggler and a man with performing dogs, and then "Miss O'Grady" was announced.

"English," said Cartwright, turning to the programme.

"She may even be Irish," said Maxell dryly. The wheezy little orchestra played a few bars and the girl came on. She was pretty – there was no doubt about that – and of a prettiness which satisfied both men. She was also British or American, for the song she sang was in a French with which both men were familiar.

"It is horrible to see an English girl in a place like this and in such company," said Maxell.

Cartwright nodded.

"I wonder where she's staying," he asked, half to himself, and a contemptuous little smile curled Maxell's lips.

"Are you going to rescue her from her infamous surroundings?" he asked, and Cartwright snapped round on him.

"I wish to heaven you wouldn't be sarcastic, Maxell. That's twice this evening–"

"Sorry," said the other, snicking off the ash of his cigar. "I am in a cynical mood tonight."

He raised his hands to applaud the girl as she bowed herself from the stage, and glanced round the house. Three boxes away was a small party of men, whom he judged were the sons of prosperous members of the Spanish colony. Their fingers flashed with diamonds, their cigarettes burnt from jewelled holders. Cartwright followed the direction of the other's eyes.

"She's made a hit, that Miss O'Grady," he said. "These fellows will be tumbling over one another to present her with verbal bouquets. I wonder where she lives!" he said again.

Presently the young men rose in a body and left the box, and Cartwright grinned.

"Do you mind hanging on here whilst I go outside?"

"Not a bit," said the other. "Where are you off to? To find out where she lives?"

"There you go again," grumbled Cartwright. "I think Tangier makes you liverish."

When he had got to the promenade, the men had disappeared, but a question directed to the head attendant revealed, as he had expected, the objective of the little party at the stage door.

The stage door was reached from the outside of the theatre and involved a journey over rubble and brick heaps. Presently he came to an open doorway, where sat a solitary half-caste smoking a pipe and reading an old *Heraldo*.

"Oh, *hombre*," said Cartwright in Spanish, "have you seen my three friends come in here?"

"Yes, Señor," nodded the man; "they have just entered."

He indicated the direction, which lay through a dark and smelly passage.

Cartwright walked along this stuffy hallway, and, turning the corner, came upon an interesting group gathered about a closed door, against which one, and the least sober, of the party was hammering. Near by stood a small, stout man in soiled evening dress, grinning his approval, and it was clear that the visitors were at once known and welcome.

"Open the door, my dream of joy," hiccupped the young man, hammering at the panel. "We have come to bring you homage and adoration – tell her to open the door, Jose," he addressed the manager of Tangier's theatre, and the small man minced forward and spoke in English.

"It is all right, my dear. Some friends of mine wish to see you."

A voice inside, which Cartwright recognised, answered: "I will not see them. Tell them to go away."

"You hear?" said the manager, shrugging his shoulders. "She will not see you. Now go back to your seats and let me persuade her."

"Señor!" He raised his eyebrows to the unexpected apparition of Cartwright. "What are you doing here?"

"I have come to see my friend," said Cartwright, "Miss O'Grady."

"It is forbidden to enter the theatre through the saloon of artistes," said the small man pompously. "If Miss O'Grady is your friend, you must wait for her until the performance is over."

Cartwright took no notice. He was a tall man of athletic build, and shouldering his way past the others with no difficulty, he tapped on the panel.

"Miss O'Grady," he said, "here is an English visitor wants to see you!"

"English?" said the voice. "Come in for the love of Mike!"

The door was opened, and a girl with a silk kimono pulled over her stage dress offered him a smiling welcome. The young Spaniard who had been hammering on the panel of the door would have followed, but Cartwright's arm barred him.

"Do you want this fellow?" he asked.

"Do I want him – " said Miss O'Grady bitterly, "do I want the scarlet fever or measles? You bet I don't want him. He's been pestering me ever since I've been here."

"Do you hear what the lady says?" said Cartwright, speaking in Spanish. "She does not desire your acquaintance."

"My father owns this theatre," said the young man loudly.

"Then he's got a rotten property," replied the calm Cartwright.

The Spaniard turned in a rage to his soiled satellite.

"You will put this man out at once, Jose, or there will be trouble for you."

The little man shrugged his helplessness.

"Sir," he said in English, "you see my unhappy position. The señor is the son of my proprietor and it will be bad for me if you stay. I ask you as a friend and caballero to go at once and spare me misfortune."

Cartwright looked at the girl.

"Must you go on again in this infernal place?" he asked.

She nodded, laughter and admiration in her eyes.

"What happens if you chuck this infernal job?"

"I'm fired," said the girl. "I've a ten weeks' contract with these people."

"What do you get?"

"Two hundred and fifty pesetas a week," she said contemptuously. "It's a wonderful salary, isn't it?"

He nodded.

"How many more weeks have you to go before your contract is finished?"

"Another four," she said, "we're playing in Cadiz next week, in Seville the week after, then Malaga, then Granada."

"Do you like it?"

"Like it!" the scorn in her voice was her answer.

"The dresses belong to the troupe, I guess," he said. "Get into your street clothes and I'll wait for you."

"What are you going to do?" she asked, eyeing him narrowly.

"I'll make good your lost contract," he said.

"Why?"

He shrugged his shoulders.

"I don't like to see an English girl – "

"Irish," she corrected.

"I mean Irish," he laughed. "I don't like to see an Irish girl doing this kind of thing with a lot of horrible half-breeds. You've talent enough for London or Paris. What about Paris? I know any number of people there."

"Could you get me a good engagement?" she asked eagerly.

He nodded.

"What's your name, anyway?" she demanded. "Never mind about my name. Smith, Brown, Jones, Robinson – anything you like."

It was the agitated little manager who interfered.

"Sir," he said, "you must not persuade this lady to leave the theatre. I have her under heavy penalties. I can bring her before the judge – "

"Now just forget that!" said Cartwright, "there is no judge in Tangier. She is a British subject, and the most you can do is to take her before the British Consul."

"When she returns to Spain – " said the little man growing apoplectic.

"She will not return to Spain. She will go to Gibraltar if she goes anywhere," said Cartwright, "and from Gibraltar she will be on the sea until she reaches a British port."

"I will go to the Spanish Consul," screamed the little manager, clawing the air. "I will not be robbed. You shall not interfere with my business, you – "

Much of this, thought Cartwright, was intended for the glowering young Spaniard who stood in the background. He went outside, closed the door and stood with his back toward it. On a whispered instruction from his employer's son, whose hands were now flickering fire as he gesticulated in his excitement, Jose the manager disappeared, and returned a few minutes later with two stalwart stage hands.

"Will you leave this theatre at once and quietly?" demanded the foaming manager.

"I will not leave the theatre until I am ready," said Cartwright, "and if I leave otherwise, I shall certainly not leave quietly."

The manager stood back with a melodramatic gesture.

"Eject the caballero," he said finally.

The two men hesitated. Then one came forward.

"The señor must leave," he said.

"In good time, my friend," replied Cartwright.

A hand gripped his arm, but instantly he had shaken free, and had driven with all his strength at the man's jaw. The stage hand dropped like a log. He pushed at the door behind him.

"Put your kimono over your things," he said quickly. "You can send the stage kit back tomorrow. There is going to be a rough house."

"All right," said a voice behind him, and the girl slipped out, still in her kimono and carrying a bundle of clothes under her arm.

"You know the way out? I'll follow you. Now, Jose," he said flippantly, "I'm going – quietly."

2

He left behind him a pandemonium of sound and a scintillation of flickering diamonds. He found the girl waiting for him in the darkness.

"Br-r-r! It's cold!" she shivered.

"Where are you staying?" he asked.

"At the little hotel opposite the British Consulate," she said. "It isn't much of a place, but it was the only room I could get – at the price."

"You'd better not go there," he said. "I'll send for your boxes in the morning. Give me those clothes."

He took them from her and put them under his arm, and she fell in by his side.

"I am glad to be out of it," she said breathlessly, taking his arm; "it's a dog's life. I was going to quit tomorrow. Those boys have been following me round ever since I came to Tangier. I don't think I'd better go back to my hotel, anyway," she said after a moment; "they're a pretty tough crowd, these Spaniards, and though I don't understand their beastly language, I know just what kind of happy holiday they're planning for me."

They were in the town, passing up the street of the mosque, when she asked him:

"Where are you taking me?"

"To the Continental," he said.

"Like this?" she said in dismay, and he laughed.

"I have an office in this street," he said; "you can go in and dress. I'll wait for you outside."

He showed her into the tiny room which served as the headquarters of the Angera Gold Mining Syndicate, and sat on the irregular stone steps, waiting until she was dressed. Presently she came out, a presentable and an attractive figure.

"I have just thought," he said, "that you had better go to the Central – I am staying at the Continental and it wouldn't look nice."

"I've been thinking something of the sort myself," she said. "What about my broken engagement? Were you joking when you said you would pay? I hate talking about money, but I am broke – Jose owes me a week's salary."

"I'll make good the money tomorrow," he said. "I can give you a tenner now."

"What is the idea?" she asked him again. "I've read a lot of books, and I know the knight errant business backwards. You don't strike me as being a something-for-nothing man."

"I'm not," he said coolly. "It occurred to me when I saw you on the stage, that you might be useful. I want a person in Paris I can trust – somebody who could look after my interests."

"I'm not a business woman," she said quickly. "I hate business."

"Business is done by men," said he significantly. "And there are a few men I want you to keep track of. Do you understand that?"

She nodded.

"I see," she said at last. "It is better than I thought."

He did not trouble to ask her what she had thought, or what she imagined he had planned, but saw her into the hotel, arranged for a room, and walked slowly back to the Continental. He was in the vestibule of that hotel before he remembered that he had left an eminent King's Counsel and Member of Parliament smoking his cigar in a *loge* of the Tangier circus.

"I missed you," said Maxell the next morning. "When you remembered and came to pick me up, I was on my way back – we must have passed somewhere in the little Sok. What happened last night?"

"Nothing much," said Cartwright airily. "I went round and saw the girl. She was very amusing."

"How amusing?" asked the other curiously.

"Oh, just amusing." Vaguely: "I found her annoyed by the attention which was being paid to her by a veritable Spanish hidalgo."

"And you sailed in and rescued her, eh?" said Maxell. "And what happened to her after she was rescued?"

"I saw her home to her hotel, and there the matter ended. By the way, she leaves by the *Gibel Musa* for Gibraltar this morning."

"Hm!" Maxell looked absently at the letter he had in his hand, folded it and put it away.

"Is the mail in?" asked Cartwright, interested, and Maxell nodded.

"I suppose you've had your daily letter from your kiddie?"

Maxell smiled.

"Yes," he said, "it is not a baby letter, but it is very amusing."

"How old is she?" asked Cartwright.

"She must be nine or ten," said the other.

"I wonder if it is just coincidence, or whether it is fate," mused Cartwright.

"What is a coincidence?" asked the other.

"The fact that you've got a kid to look after, and I'm in a sort of way responsible for a bright lad. Mine is less interesting than yours, I think. Anyway, he's a boy and a sort of cousin. He has two fool parents who were born to slavery – the sort of people who are content to work for somebody all their lives and regard revolt against their condition as an act of impiety. I've only seen the kid once, and he struck me as the sort who might break loose from that kind of life and take a chance. Otherwise, I wouldn't have interested myself in him."

"How far does your interest extend?" asked Maxell curiously. "You're not the sort of person, I should imagine, who would take up the unfortunate poor as a hobby."

"Not a something-for-nothing man, in fact," laughed Cartwright. "I've been told that twice in twenty-four hours."

"Who was the other person – the actress?"

Cartwright roared with laughter and slapped the other on the knee.

"You're a good guesser," he said. "No, I am not a something-for-nothing person. I'm one of those optimists who plant fir cones so that I shall have some good firewood for my old age. I don't know what sort of a man Timothy will make, but, as I say, he shapes good, and anyway, you and I are in the same boat."

"Except this," said Maxell, "that from what you say, you aren't particularly interested in your protégé, and you don't really care whether he shapes good or shapes bad."

"That's true," admitted Cartwright. "He's an experiment."

"My little girl is something more than that," said Maxell quietly; "she's the only living thing I have any real affection for – she is my dead brother's child."

"Your niece, eh? Well, that gives you an interest which I have not. I never had a niece and I should just hate to be called uncle, anyway."

Their conversation was interrupted at this point by the arrival of a small man dressed in his best clothes. On his brow was a frown which was intended to be terrible, but was slightly amusing. Jose Ferreira had dressed and prepared himself for an interview which, as he had described to his friends, could not fail to be at once "terrifying and vital." For, as he had said: "This man has sliced my life!"

He began his speech to Cartwright as he had rehearsed it.

"*Estoy indignado* – "

But Cartwright cut him short with an expression of mock fear. "*Horroroso!* You are indignant, are you? Well, come, little man, and tell me why you are indignant."

"Señor," said the man solemnly, "you have put upon me a humiliation and a shame which all my life I shall regret."

The conversation was in Spanish, but Maxell was an excellent Spanish scholar.

"What's the trouble?" he asked, before Jose, still labouring under the sense of his wrongs, could get going again.

"Listen to him and discover," mocked Cartwright. "I have taken from his incomparable company its joy and its gem."

"In other words, the amiable Miss O'Grady," said Maxell.

"Yes, yes, señor," broke in Jose. "For me it is ruin! The money I have spent to make my company perfect! It is financed by one who is the greatest man in Tangier and it is his son who tells me that, unless I bring back this lady – for me there is the street and the gutter," he wept.

Maxell looked slyly at his companion.

"There's another chance for you to plant a fir cone," he said. "Can't you find some use for this gentleman?"

But Cartwright was not smiling.

"Señor Ferreira," he said crisply, "you are, as all Spain knows, a thief and a rogue. If you associate with bigger thieves and bigger scoundrels, that is your business. I can only tell you that you may think yourself lucky I did not bring this case before the Spanish Consul. I assure you, you would never have put your foot in Tangier again after the stories I have heard about you."

The little Spaniard was open-mouthed and impressed. He was also a little frightened. Cartwright's accusation had been at a venture, but he argued that it was scarcely likely that, in an establishment of the description which Mr Ferreira controlled, there could have been no incidents which reflected upon the manager.

"Everything which is said about me is a lie!" said the little man vigorously. "I have lived a life of the highest virtue! Today I complain to the British Consul, and we shall see!"

"Complain," said Cartwright.

"This chance I will give you." Señor Ferreira wagged a fat, stumpy finger. "Restore to me Miss O'Grady, and the matter shall go no farther."

"Miss O'Grady has left Tangier," said the other calmly, "so it is clear to you that I cannot restore her."

"She has not left," vociferated the Spaniard. "We had a man to watch the boat leaving for the *Gibel Musa* and she did not leave the pier."

"She left the beach," explained Cartwright patiently; "she was rowed out by a boatman from the Cecil. At this moment she is half way to Gibraltar."

Mr Ferreira groaned.

"It is ruin for me," he said. "Perhaps for you also," he added ominously. "I can do no less than depart for Paris to lay this matter before my excellent patron, Señor Don – "

Cartwright jerked his head to the door.

"Get out," he said, and turned his attention to the newspaper which he had picked up from the table.

Maxell waited until the little man had gone, still seething with his "indignado," then turned to Cartwright.

"This is rather a serious matter, Cartwright; what has happened to the girl?"

"Didn't you hear? I have sent her to Gibraltar," said Cartwright. "I wouldn't leave a dog in that company. And from Gibraltar she goes home by the first P&O," he said briefly.

"Hm!" said Maxell for the second time.

"What the devil are you 'hming' about?" snarled his companion. "The girl is gone. I shall not see her again. It was an act of charity. Do you disapprove?"

"I'm sorry," said Maxell. "I didn't know you felt so bad about it. No, I think you've done the girl a very good turn. But in these days one doesn't expect – "

"Blessed is he that expecteth nothing, Maxell," said Cartwright sententiously, "for he shall not be disappointed. I don't suppose that the proprietor, whoever he is, cares a snap of his fingers about the matter – it is his infernal son who will fire the adorable Jose."

That afternoon the two men had an interview on the outskirts of the town with a very plainly dressed Moor, who came to them so cautiously that the observers might have been pardoned if they thought he was a criminal. In the eyes of the divine rulers of Morocco he was something more than a criminal, because he was an emissary of El Mograb, the Pretender. There was a price upon the messenger's head, and his caution was, therefore, commendable. He brought a letter from El Mograb to Cartwright, and it was a message of cheer.

Maxell and his friend had gone out early in the afternoon and had waited two hours under a scorching sun for the courier to arrive. For a man of law, the fact that he was coquetting with the Sultan's enemy did not distress Maxell, who knew the history of the country too well to worry very much about Sultan or Pretender. The Sultan's reign, marked with the turbulence of people and the self-indulgence of monarch, was already doomed. His uncle, El Mograb, a born leader of men and captain of seven thousand well-armed soldiers, was but waiting the psychological moment to strike; and Adbul, with his motor-cars and brass bedstead, his geegaws and his frippery, would disappear into the limbo which is especially reserved for extravagant and unstable rulers.

The news from El Mograb was good. It reconfirmed the concession which one of his shereefs had made on his behalf, and sent a message in flowery Arabic – a message of thanks to the man who had supplied him with the very necessary rifles.

"That was news to me," said Cartwright as they rode back to the town. "I didn't know you were gun-running, Maxell, or that you were so solid with El Mograb."

"I like El Mograb," said Maxell. "He's one of the many Moors who have impressed me. You mustn't forget that I have been visiting Morocco since I was a boy and most of the chiefs are known to me personally. I knew El Mograb's brother, who was killed at Tetuan, and when he was a favourite in court circles he entertained me at Fez."

"What is his word worth?" asked Cartwright carelessly.

"It is worth all the contracts that ever went to Somerset House for stamping," said the other with emphasis. "I think you can go ahead with your scheme."

Cartwright nodded.

"I'll go back to London and raise the money," he said. "We shall want a couple of millions eventually, but half a million will do to go on with. You had better be with me in the big scheme, Maxell. There is nothing to lose for you. You'll be in on the ground floor. What is the good of your pottering about with your little Company – I mean the Parent Company?"

"I have faith in that," said Maxell, "I know just the amount of my indebtedness."

"You're a fool," said the other shortly. "The big scheme may mean millions to you, and I shall want your help and guidance."

Maxell hesitated. The lure was dazzling, the prize was immense. But it meant risks which he was not prepared to take. He knew something of Cartwright's financial methods; he had seen them in their working, and had done not a little on one occasion to save Cartwright from the consequences of his own cleverness. Yet, as he argued, Cartwright would have no difficulty in raising the money from the general public, and his presence on the board would certainly be a guarantee against his companion departing from the narrow path.

Although it was not generally known that he was associated in any of Cartwright's enterprises, there had been a whisper of an inquiry in influential quarters, and it had been hinted to him that, on the whole, it would be better if he kept himself aloof from the gentleman who, admirable business man as he was, had a passion for enterprises which occasionally verged upon the illegal. But those influential quarters had not whispered anything in the shape of a definite promise that his welfare was entirely in their keeping and that his future would not be overlooked.

He was an ambitious man, but his ambitions ran in realisable directions. The services he had rendered to the Government were such as deserved a recognition, and the only question was what form that recognition would take? His knowledge of languages qualified him for an important appointment under the Foreign Office; but the Foreign Office was a close preserve and difficult to break into. There were too many permanent officials who regarded the service as a family affair, and were jealous of patronage outside their own charmed circle.

He went in to lunch that day to find Cartwright reading a telegram which he folded up and put into his pocket upon the other's appearance.

"My little friend has arrived in Gibraltar," said Cartwright.

Maxell looked at him curiously.

"What happens now?" he demanded.

"Oh, I'm sending her home."

Cartwright's voice was brisk and he spoke in the manner of a man referring to a topic too unimportant to be discussed.

"And after?" pursued Maxell, and the other shrugged his shoulders.

"I have given her a letter of introduction to a friend of mine," he said carelessly. "I have one or two theatrical interests in town."

Maxell said nothing, and could have dismissed the matter as lightly as his companion, for the girl's future scarcely interested him.

She had been but a figure on the stage; her personality, her very appearance, left no definite impression. But if he was not interested in the girl, he was interested in Cartwright's private mind. Here was a man of whom he could not know too much. And somehow he felt that he had hardly cracked the surface of Cartwright's character though he had known him for years, and though they were working together to a common end.

The way of a man with a maid is wonderful, but it is also instructive to the cold-blooded onlooker, who discovers in that way a kind of creature he has never met before; a new man, so entirely different from the familiar being he had met in club or drawing-room as to be almost unrecognisable. And he wanted to know just this side of Cartwright, because it was the side on which he had scarcely any information.

"I suppose you won't see her again?" he said, playing with his knife and looking abstractedly out of the window.

"I shouldn't think so," said Cartwright, and then, with a sudden irritation: "What the devil are you driving at, Maxell? I may see the girl – I go to music-halls, and it is hardly likely I should miss her. Naturally I am interested in the lady I have rescued from this kind of thing" – he waved his hand vaguely toward Tangier Bay – "and she may be useful. You don't mean to say *you're* struck on her?"

He tried to carry war into the enemy's camp and failed, for Maxell's blue eyes met his steadily.

"I hardly know what she looks like," he said, "and I am not likely to fall in love with a lady who left absolutely no impression upon me." He left next day on the boat for Cadiz, en route to Paris and London, and he and Cartwright had as a fellow-passenger a shabby little man whose belongings were packed in an American-cloth suit-case inscribed in flourishing capitals, evidently by the owner, "Jose Ferreira."

Mr Ferreira spent most of his time on the ship's deck, biting his nails and enlarging his grievance against the unconscious Cartwright.

3

Maxell did not stay many hours in Paris. The Sud Express landed him in the French capital at seven in the morning. He left Paris by the midday train for London. The Long Vacation was drawing to an end, and there were briefs of certain importance requiring examination. There was also a consultation with the Attorney-General on an interpretation of a clause in the new Shipping Act, and he was also due to address his constituents before the reassembling of Parliament.

He might ruminate in vain to find one attractive feature of his programme. Parliament wearied him, and the ordinary practices of the law no longer gave him pleasure.

There was an interest in the work he was doing for the Government, and if he had the faintest hint of pleasure in his immediate prospects, the cause was to be found in the vexed problems centring about this new, and loosely drawn, shipping law. It was a measure which had been passed in a hurry, and when the acid test of litigation had been applied, some of its weak points had been discovered.

The weakest of these points was one affecting the load-line. In an action heard before a High Court Judge, the doubtful clause had been interpreted so as to render the Act a dead letter; and there were particular and especial Governmental reasons why the appeal which the Government had made from the verdict of the lower Court should upset that decision.

There is no need to give the particulars of the great dispute, which arose over the three words "or otherwise loaded," and it is only necessary to say that, before he had reached London, Mr Maxell had discovered a way for the Government out of their difficulty.

It was this opinion which he delivered to a relieved Attorney-General, and, with the new argument, the Government were able to present so strong a case to the Court of Appeal, that a month after his return the verdict of the lower Court was reversed.

"And," said the Attorney-General, "the devils can take it to the House of Lords now and still lose – thanks to your brain wave, Maxell!"

They were smoking in the Crown Room at the Law Courts after the decision had been delivered.

"Where have you been for your holiday, by the way?" asked the Attorney suddenly.

"Morocco," replied the other.

"Morocco?" The Attorney nodded thoughtfully. "Did you hear anything of friend Cartwright?" he asked.

"We were staying at the same hotel," replied Maxell.

"A weird person," said the thoughtful Attorney. "A very curious man – what a Chancellor that fellow would make!"

"He never struck me that way," smiled Maxell.

"Do you know him well – I mean, are you a particular friend of his?" demanded the Attorney.

"No," said Maxell indifferently. "I know him – so many men in the law know him."

"You're not by any chance associating with him in business now, are you?"

"No," said Maxell promptly.

It was a lie and he knew it was a lie. It was told deliberately from the desire to stand well in the eyes of his friends. He knew Cartwright's reputation well enough, and just how he was regarded by the party whom he had served for three years. Cartwright had been Member for a London borough, but had resigned. "Pressure of business" was the excuse he gave, but there were people who said that it was owing to the pressure of the Party Whips, who smelt a somewhat unsavoury case coming into Court with Cartwright figuring prominently.

There is no way of proving or disproving the statement, because the case in which Cartwright most decidedly was interested was withdrawn from the list at the last moment. The uncharitable say that it cost Cartwright a small fortune to bring about this withdrawal, and certainly one of the ladies interested (she was a small-part actress at the Hippoceus) gave up her stage work and had been living in affluence ever since. Cartwright pooh-poohed the suggestion that the case held anything sensational – but he did not enter political life again.

"I am glad you're not associated with him," said the Attorney simply. "He's an awfully nice fellow and I suppose he is as straight and as sound as the best man in the City. But he's a shifty fellow – just a little bit" – he hesitated – "a little wrong. You understand, Maxell – or shall we say slightly shop-soiled?"

"He is certainly a brilliant man," said Maxell, not desirous of defending his friend too vigorously.

"Yes, I suppose he is," admitted the Attorney. "All men like that are brilliant. What a pity his genius does not run in a smooth channel, but must follow the course of a burning cracker, here, there and everywhere, exploding at every turn!"

He slipped down from the table, on the edge of which he had been sitting and pulled off his robe.

"I'm glad to know you're not associated with Cartwright, anyway," he said.

Maxell did not attempt to probe beneath the surface of his twice-repeated remark.

He went back to Cavendish Square to his flat and to a tiny, solemn-eyed little girl who had been brought up from Hindhead that day on her monthly visit to "Uncle Max."

Cartwright had not accompanied his friend to England, and with good reasons. A great deal of his work was carried out in Paris, where he had an important financial backing. He occupied a flat overlooking the imposing, but none too convenient, Avenue of the Grand Army. His home was at the unfashionable end of this interminable thoroughfare, which meant that his rooms were larger and his rent cheaper, and that he was freer from observation than he would have been had he lived according to his means or station in a luxurious flat nearer the Etoile.

He had a board meeting to attend, an informal board meeting, it is true, but none the less important.

Cartwright was the chairman and managing director of the London and Paris Gold Syndicate, a flourishing concern which held big blocks of shares in various land and gold-mining companies, and controlled three mines of its own on the West Rand. Though a Company drawing a modest revenue from its Johannesburg property, its operations were not confined to gold development pure and simple. It was, in fact, an outside broker's on a grand scale. It gambled heavily and gambled wisely. The shareholders seldom received less than a twelve and a half per cent dividend, and there were years when in addition it paid a bonus equal to its own share capital.

It numbered its clients at one hundred and fifty thousand, the majority being small people who preferred speculation to investment – country parsons, doctors and the small gamblers who lived fearfully on the fringe of high finance. The shares were at a premium and Cartwright's interest brought him a considerable sum annually. What probably attracted the little speculator was the knowledge of the Company's reserve, which stood in the balance-sheet at a respectable figure. It was the question of these reserves that occupied the attention of the four quiet men who met informally in the room of a Paris hotel.

There were three to one against Cartwright, because none of his companions could see eye to eye with him.

"It is too dangerous, M. Cartwright," said Gribber, whose nationality was suspect; "our risks are already high and we cannot afford, in my judgment, to extend them. The money would be subscribed over and over again if you went to the English public."

Cartwright frowned.

"Why shouldn't we make the profit?" he asked; "we could borrow from our reserve."

"That we can't touch!" interrupted the cautious Gribber, shaking his head violently. "My faith, no, we cannot touch that! For it is certain that the lean years will come when our clients will require their dividends."

Cartwright did not pursue the subject. There were other ways of financing his Moorish scheme.

The Benson Syndicate, for example.

He spoke eloquently of this new venture, which was to have its headquarters in Paris, and would be under the eye of his sceptical co-directors. He mentioned names glibly and easily – names that carried weight in the financial world. The three men agreed that the Benson Syndicate had the appearance of a safe investment.

More important was the business which brought Alfred Cartwright to the St Lazare Station to meet a passenger a week later.

She sprang from the train and looked round with doubting face, which lighted the moment she saw the saturnine Cartwright.

"My! I am relieved," she said. "I was scared to think you wouldn't be here to meet me, and I'd only got a few pounds left."

"You got my wire?" he asked, and she smiled, showing two rows of pearly teeth.

"I'm still mystified," she said. "What is it you want me to do in Paris?"

"Let us eat first and talk afterwards," he said. "You must be hungry."

"I'm starving!" she laughed.

He had a car waiting for her, and whisked her off to a little street leading from the Boulevard des Italiens, where one of the best restaurants in Paris is situated. The girl looked about her with an approving air. The gaiety and luxury of the place appealed to her.

"My word!" she said enviously; "do you come to lunch here every day?"

"Do you know this place?" he asked.

"I've seen it," she admitted, "but a three franc dinner at Duval's has been my limit so far."

She told him how she had come to the Continent as a dancer, and had "starred" in a tiny little cabaret in Montmartre as one of the "dashing Sisters Jones," before she had been seen by the impresario who was recruiting material for his tour through the Levant.

Cartwright judged her to be nineteen, knew her to be extremely pretty, and guessed that, under certain conditions, she would be presentable even to the best of the circles in which he moved. He wondered, with a grim smile, what Maxell, that austere and fastidious man, would say if he knew that the girl was with him in Paris. Would Maxell accept her? He thought not. Maxell was a touch strait-laced and in some ways was a bore. But Maxell was necessary. He was a brilliant lawyer, and moreover stood well with the Government, and there might come a time when Maxell would be immensely useful. He could well afford to give the lawyer a slice of the pickings he intended making, because Maxell's wants were few and his ambitions on the modest side.

Cartwright thought in millions. Maxell was a five-figure man. If all went well with Cartwright's scheme, undoubtedly he could well afford the five figures.

"What happened to your friend?" asked the girl, as though divining his thoughts: "The man you told me I was to keep away from. Why didn't you want him to see me?"

Cartwright shrugged his shoulders.

"Does it really matter?" he asked; "he's in England, anyway."

"Who is he?" She was curious.

"Oh, a friend of mine."

"And who are you?" she asked, facing him squarely. "If I'm going to see anything of you in Paris, that Smith, Brown or Robinson business isn't quite good enough. You've been decent to me, but I want to know who I'm working for, and what is the kind of work you want me to do."

Cartwright pinched his neck – a nervous little trick of his when he was thinking.

"I have business interests here," he said.

"You don't want me for an office?" she asked suspiciously. "My education is perfectly rotten."

He shook his head.

"No, I don't want you for an office," he replied with a smile. "And yet in a sense I want you to do office work. I have a little syndicate here, which is known as the Benson Syndicate. Benson is my name – "

"Or the name you go by," she said quickly, and he laughed.

"How sharp you are! Well, I don't suppose O'Grady is your name, if it comes to that."

She made no reply and he went on:

"I want somebody in Paris I can rely upon; somebody who will receive money, transmit it to the Benson Syndicate, and reinvest that money in such concerns as I shall indicate."

"Don't use long words," she said. "How do you know I'm not going to rob you? Nobody's ever trusted me with money before."

He might have told her that she would not be trusted with a great deal at a time and that she would be carefully watched. He preferred, however, an explanation more flattering to his new assistant. And not only was it flattering, but it contained a big grain of truth, expressing, to an extent, Alfred Cartwright's creed.

"Women are more honest than men," he said. "I should think twice before I put a man – even my best friend – in the position I'm putting you. It will be a simple matter, and I shall pay you well. You can live at one of the best hotels – in fact, it is absolutely necessary that you should. You may" – he hesitated – "you may be Madam Benson, a rich Englishwoman."

She looked at him from under perplexed brows.

"What is the good of asking me to do that?" she said in a tone of disappointment. "I thought you were going to give me a job I could do. I'm a fool at business."

"You can remain a fool," he said coolly. "There's nothing to do except carry out a certain routine, which I shall explain to you so that you can't possibly make a mistake. Here is a job which gives you plenty of time, pays you well, gives you good clothes and an auto. Now, are you going to be a sensible girl and take it?"

She thought a moment, then nodded.

"If it means lunching here every day, I'll take it," she said decidedly.

Thus was formed the remarkable Benson Syndicate, about which so much has been written, and so many theories evolved. For, if the truth be told, the Benson Syndicate had no existence until Cartwright called it into being in Ciro's Restaurant. It was born of the opposition he had received, and its creation was hastened by certain disquieting telegrams which arrived almost every hour from London.

Cartwright was, as has been said, a man of many interests. The door-plate of his office in Victoria Street, London, was covered with the names of the companies which had their headquarters in the ornate suite which he occupied. There were two other suites of offices in the City of London for which Mr Cartwright paid the rent, although he did not pay it in his own name. There were syndicates and companies innumerable, Development Syndicates, Exploitation Companies, Financial and Mining Companies, all duly registered and all keeping one solicitor busy; for the Companies Acts are tricky, and Cartwright was too clever a man to contravene minor regulations.

And to all these companies there were shareholders; some of them contented, some – the majority – wholly dissatisfied with their lot, and quite a large number who were wont to show their share certificates to their friends as curiosities, and tell them the sad story of how they were inveigled into investment.

Only a clever company lawyer can describe in detail the tortuous character of Cartwright's system of finance. It involved loans from one company to another, very often on the security of shares in a third company; it involved a system of overdrafts, drawn in favour of some weakly member of his family, secured by the assets of one which could show a bold face to the world, and was even quoted in the Stock Exchange list; and divers other complicated transactions, which only the expert mathematician could follow.

Cartwright was a rich man, accounted a millionaire by his friends; but he was that type of millionaire who was never at a loss for a thousand, but who was generally hard up for ten thousand. He came to London much against his will, in response to an urgent telegram, and, having cleared the difficulties which his subordinates had found insuperable, he had a few hours to attend to his private affairs before he took the train back to Paris.

His secretary produced a heap of small bills requiring settlement, and going through these, he paused before one printed slip, and frowned.

"That boy's school fees weren't paid last term," he said.

"No, sir," said the secretary. "If you remember, I mentioned the matter to you when you were in London last. I was taking upon myself the responsibility of paying the fees, if you hadn't returned. The boy is coming up today, by the way, sir, to be measured for some clothes."

"Coming here?" asked Mr Cartwright, interested.

"Yes, sir."

Cartwright picked up the bill.

"T A C Anderson," he read. "What does T A C stand for – 'Take A Chance'?"

"I understood he was named after you – Timothy Alfred Cartwright," said the secretary.

"Yes; of course," Cartwright grinned. "Still, Take A Chance isn't a bad name for a kid. When is he arriving?"

"He ought to be here now," said the man, looking at his watch. "I'll go out and see."

He disappeared into the outer office, and presently returned.

"The boy is here, sir," he said. "Would you like to see him?"

"Bring him in," said Cartwright. "I'd like to meet this nephew, or cousin, or whatever he is."

He wondered vaguely what had induced him to take upon himself the responsibility of the small child, and with remorseless judgment analysed the reason as being personal vanity.

The door opened and a child strode in. "Strode" is the only word to describe the quick, decisive movement of the bright-eyed lad who looked with unflinching eye at Cartwright. Cartwright did not look at his clothes, but at the grey, clear eyes, the firm mouth, extraordinarily firm for a boy of fourteen, and the capable and not over-clean hands.

"Sit down, son," said Cartwright. "So you're my nephew."

"Cousin, I think," said the boy, critically examining the contents of Cartwright's table. "You're Cousin Alfred, aren't you?"

"Oh, I'm a cousin, am I? Yes, I suppose I am," said Cartwright, amused.

"I say," said the boy, "is that the school bill? The Head has been rather baity about that."

" 'Baity'?" said the puzzled Cartwright. "That's a new one on me."

"Shirty," said the boy calmly. "Annoyed, I suppose, is the correct word."

Cartwright chuckled.

"What do you want to be?" he asked.

"A financier," said T A C Anderson promptly.

He seated himself, leant his elbow on the desk and his head on his hand, his eyes never leaving Cartwright.

"I think that's a great scheme – finance," he said. "I'm a whale at mathematics."

"What particular branch of finance?" asked Cartwright with a smile.

"Other people's finance," said the boy promptly; "the same business as yours."

Cartwright threw back his head and laughed.

"And do you think you'd be able to keep twenty companies in the air at the same time?" he said.

"In the air?" the boy frowned. "Oh, you mean going all at once? Rather! Anyway, I'd take a chance."

The phrase struck Cartwright.

"Take a chance? That's curious. I called you Take A Chance Anderson just before you came in."

"Oh, they all call me that," said the boy indifferently. "You see, they're bound to stick a label on to a fellow with an initial like mine.

Some of them call me 'Tin and Copper Anderson,' but most of them – the other name."

"You're a rum kid," said his cousin. "You can come to lunch with me."

4

Mr Alfred Cartwright had the enviable faculty of placing outside of his mind all subjects and persons which were unpleasant to think upon. Possessing this power, he could as lightly dismiss the memory of responsibilities, pleasant or unpleasant. He had scarcely left London before he had waived Master T A C Anderson into oblivion. To do him justice, he had certainly speculated vaguely upon assuring his cousin's future; but his mind was so completely occupied with his own that there was really not room for both – and Take A Chance Anderson had to go.

He reached Paris by the evening train, and drove straight to the apartment he had taken for his new protégée. He found her installed in a very comfortable flat on the unfashionable side of the Seine, and was welcomed with relief.

Miss Sadie O'Grady had not entirely overcome her suspicions of the bona fides of her new-found acquaintance. Yet, since he had not made love to her, but, on the contrary, had made it very clear that the part he expected her to play in his schemes involved no loss of self-respect, she was becoming reconciled to a relationship which, to say the least, was a strange one. She had established herself in a third-floor office on one of the boulevards, an uncomfortable and unaccustomed figure in an environment which was wholly foreign to her experience, though there was no need for her embarrassment, since she constituted the whole of the staff, and the callers were confined to the postman and the concierge who acted as office-cleaner.

She was to learn, however, that a daily attendance at her "bureau" did not constitute the whole of her duties, or fulfil all Cartwright's requirements.

It was not until after dinner that night that Cartwright revealed himself.

"Sadie, my young friend," he said, between puffs of his cigar, "I am going to tell you just what I want you to do."

"I thought I knew," she said, on her guard, and he laughed softly.

"You'll never quite know what I want you to do," he said frankly, "until I tell you. Now, I'm putting it to you very straight. I want nothing from you except service. And the service I require is of a kind which you need not hesitate to give me. You're an actress, and I can speak to you more plainly than I could to some unsophisticated girl."

She wondered what was coming, but had not long to wait.

"I will tell you something," he said, "which is really more important than my name, about which you showed so much curiosity. There is a man in this city whom I want to get at."

"How do you mean?" she asked suspiciously.

"He is a man who has it in his power to ruin me – a drunken sot of a fellow, without brain or imagination."

He went on to explain briefly that he himself was a company promoter, and that he had an interest in a mine, as yet unproved, in Morocco.

"That is why you were there?" she nodded.

"That is exactly why," replied Cartwright. "Unfortunately, right in the midst of the ground which I have either bought or secured mineral rights over, is a block of land which is the property of this man. He is a Spaniard – do you speak Spanish?"

"A little," she admitted, "but it is precious little!"

"It doesn't matter," Cartwright shook his head. "He speaks English very well. Now, this land is absolutely valueless to the man, but every attempt I have made to buy it has been unsuccessful, and it is vitally necessary at this moment, when I am floating a company to develop the property, that his claims should be included in my properties."

"What is his name?" asked the girl.

"Brigot," replied Cartwright.

"Brigot?" repeated Sadie O'Grady thoughtfully. "I seem to have heard that name before."

"It is pretty common in France, but not so common in Spain," said Mr Cartwright.

"And what am I to do?" asked the girl again.

"I will get you an introduction to him," said Cartwright; "he's a man with a fine eye for beauty, and in the hands of a clever girl could be wound round her little finger."

The girl nodded.

"I see what you mean," she said, "but nothing doing!"

"Wait!" said Cartwright. "I have told you that it is necessary for me to acquire this property. I am taking you into my confidence, and I know that you will respect that confidence. I am willing to pay any reasonable sum, and I neither want you to steal it nor make any personal sacrifice to serve my ends. I am willing to pay, and pay heavily."

"What do you call heavily?" asked the girl coolly.

"For the property twenty thousand – for you ten thousand pounds," suggested Cartwright, and the girl nodded.

"That's got me," she said. "Tell me what your plan is."

"My plan is this," said Cartwright. "You will appear to Señor Brigot – I will arrange that – as a wealthy young American lady who has been spending the winter in Morocco. His property follows a little wooded hill, one of the prettiest formations of its kind in the Angera country. You must rave about that hill, never cease speaking of its beauty and its attractiveness; and you must tell him that you would give anything in the world if you could build a house amidst that beautiful scenery – do you understand me?"

The girl nodded again.

"Brigot is a man somewhat susceptible to feminine charms," Cartwright went on, "and, unless I am greatly mistaken, he will in one of his obliging moods, offer you the land at a nominal figure, particularly as he has been bitterly disappointed in his attempt to find gold."

"I don't like it," said the girl after consideration. "You promised me that if I came to Paris you would get me a job in one of the theatres. That is what I am after, and the only thing I am fit for. The other business doesn't seem decent – "

"Ten thousand pounds!" murmured Cartwright.

"It is a lot," agreed the girl, "but how am I coming out of this business? I come out hopelessly compromised."

Cartwright shrugged his shoulders with a deprecating smile.

"My dear girl – " he began.

"Wait a moment," she said quietly; "let's have a clear understanding. You don't expect me to walk up to Señor Brigot the first time I meet him, or even the second, and say: 'You've a very nice property. What will you sell it for? That is not the kind of transaction you expect me to conduct, is it?"

"Not exactly," admitted Cartwright.

"It means just a little more than you say," said the girl; "it means dinners and suppers and hand-holdings and stringing him along. And after it is all over, where am I? I've got as much respect for my character as you have for yours, Mr Mysterious. I want to come out well in this business as you do, and I don't want to leave my name behind, or be known in Paris – which is the world – as a decoy duck. I'd do an awful lot to please you, because I like you and because you've been decent to me. But 'an awful lot' does not mean making me so cheap that I am left in the slightly-soiled basket. Do you understand what I mean?"

"Perfectly," said Cartwright, amazed at the girl's cool reasoning. He had not given her credit for any of these fine sentiments she now enunciated, and he was piqued, and at the same time a little pleased.

"When you said you'd give me ten thousand pounds," said the girl, "that sounded good. But it is not good enough. I've an idea in the back of my mind that the matter is a much bigger one for you than you've told me."

"How big do you imagine?" bantered Cartwright.

"I think it is big enough to ruin you," said the girl calmly, "and that you'd be willing to pay any price to get this property. Otherwise, you'd go to the man or send your lawyer in the ordinary way. Now, I don't want your ten thousand pounds, but I'm going to make a proposition to you. I've said I like you and that's no more than the truth. You told me you were a bachelor and I've told you that I'm man-free and heartfree. I don't say I love you, and I don't flatter myself that you love me. But if you want this thing to go through, and if you want me to go down in the mud to get it, you've got to pay the price – "

"And the price is – ?" asked Cartwright curiously.

"You've got to marry me," said the girl.

"Well, I'm – " Cartwright could only gasp his admiration; and then he began to laugh, at first quietly, and then, as the humour of the situation gained upon him, so loudly that the other patrons of the Café Scribe turned to look at him.

"It is a rum idea," he said, "but – "

"But?" she repeated, keeping her eyes on his.

He nodded to her.

"It's a bargain!" he said.

She looked at him as she put out her hand and took his, and slowly shook her head.

"My!" she said. "You want that fellow's land pretty badly, *I* know!" and Cartwright began to laugh again.

Señor Brigot lived in some style for a man who was on the verge of ruin. He had a small house at Maisons Lafitte and a flat on the Boulevard Webber. He was a heavy, tired-looking man, with a dark moustache, obviously dyed, and a short beard, bearing evidence of the same attention. M. Brigot, like Mr Cartwright, had many interests; but his chief interests were his own tastes and predilections. It was Señor Brigot's boast that, although he had lived for twenty years in Paris, he had never seen Paris between the hours of six in the morning and one in the afternoon. His breakfast hour was two o'clock. By six o'clock in the evening he was becoming interested in life; and at the hour when most people retire to rest, he was in the prime of his day.

It happened on a certain evening that M. Brigot, who usually met dinner in an amicable frame of mind, sat down at his favourite table at the Abbaye with a big frown, and answered the polite *maître d'hôtel's* cheery "Good evening" with a snarl.

Amongst his many enterprises and few possessions, and this Mr Cartwright did not know, was the proprietorship and management of a small, ramshackle wooden theatre in the town of Tangier. He was likewise interested in several cabarets throughout Spain. But what pained him most at the moment was not distressing reports from any of these, but a six-page letter received that afternoon from his son, in which the hope of the house of Brigot had explained his reasons for discharging immediately a very necessary servant. Therefore Señor Brigot swore under his breath and cursed his first-born.

Coincident with the arrival of the letter had come one Jose Ferreira, who had been detained for a week at Madrid. Señor Brigot's mind was occupied with Jose Ferreira when that worthy, smirking apologetically, as though conscious of the shabbiness of his dress-clothes, sidled into a seat on the opposite side of the table. Señor Brigot glared at him a moment, and Jose Ferreira shifted uneasily in his chair.

"If you had telegraphed to me, I would have settled the matter," said Brigot, as though carrying on a conversation which he had broken off a few minutes before. "Instead, like the fool you are, you come all the way to Paris, wasting your time in Madrid, and the first I hear of the matter is from my son."

"It was deplorable," murmured Jose, "but Don Brigot – "

"Don Brigot!" sneered the father of that worthy. "Don Brigot is a monkey! Why did you take notice of him? Have you nothing else to do in Tangier but to look after that flea-ridden theatre? Have you no other duties?"

"The young señor was emphatic," murmured the apologetic Jose. "He demanded that I should leave and what could I do?"

Brigot grunted something uncomplimentary. Whether it was intended for his son or for Ferreira, it was difficult to say. Ferreira was content to take it to himself.

Half-way through the dinner Brigot became more human.

"There will always be quarrels about women, my good Jose, and it is your business to be diplomatic," he said. "My son is a fool; but then, all young men are fools. Why should you neglect my interests because Emanuel is a bigger fool than ever? Only this week I intended travelling to Tangier with the representative of a very rich syndicate who wishes to buy my land."

"The same señor as before?" asked the interested Jose, who was not only the manager of Tangier's theatre, but was also the representative of the rusty little gold-mining company which Brigot had floated.

The other nodded.

"The same cursed Englishman," he said.

Quite unconscious of the fact that his master was cursing the very man whom Jose had most recently cursed, the little man smiled sympathetically.

"I also have a hatred of the English," he said. "With what insolence do they treat one!"

For some time M. Brigot sat in silence, but presently he wiped his mouth on his napkin, tossed down a tumbler of red wine, and crooked his finger at his companion, inviting closer attention.

"In a day, or perhaps two, I shall send you back to Tangier," he said.

"The theatre?" began Jose.

"The theatre – bah!" exclaimed the other scornfully. "A donkey-driver could look after the theatre! It is the mine!"

"The mine?" repeated the other in some astonishment.

So long had it been since a spade had been put to the ground, so long had those hopes of Brigot's been apparently dead, that the very word "mine" had ceased to be employed when referring to the property.

"My Englishman will buy it," said Brigot confidently. "I happen to know that he has taken up property in the neighbourhood, and he has already made me an offer. But such an offer! He shall pay my price, Jose," he said, nodding as he picked his teeth, "and it will be a big price, because it is desirable that I should have money."

Jose did not ask the price, but his employer saved him the trouble.

"Five million pesetas," he said confidently; for such a price the property will be sold, always providing, my friend, that we do not discover gold before the sale."

Jose smiled weakly, a circumstance which seemed to annoy his companion.

"You are a fool," said Brigot irritably; "you have no brains! You think that is a preposterous sum? Wait!"

When his subordinate's dinner was finished, Jose was dismissed peremptorily. Brigot had a round of calls to make, a succession of people to be visited; and whilst he might interview the little man at dinner without losing caste, he had no desire to take him round to his usual haunts.

It was at the Abbaye at that golden hour when the price of wine soars and all that is smartest in Paris is assembled in the big saloon, that M. Brigot, who had reached a stage of geniality, met an entrancing vision. Brigot saw the girl and her cavalier at one of the tables, and recognised in the latter a well-known man about town. The latter caught his eye and walked across to him.

"Who is your charming companion?" whispered Brigot, whose failing was, as Cartwright accurately surmised, a weakness for pretty faces.

"She is an American lady who has just come from Morocco," said the other glibly.

Cartwright had chosen Sadie O'Grady's companion very well. In a few minutes Brigot had crossed to the other table and taken a seat, was introduced, and was in that pleasant glow of mind which comes to the man of his class who is conscious of having made an impression.

This "American widow," with her queer, broken French, her beautiful eyes, and the charming distinction which goes best with good clothes, was more lovely than any woman he had ever met – so he swore to himself, as he had sworn before. The friendship progressed from day to day, and so great was the impression which the girl had made, that Brigot was seen abroad at most unusual hours.

The patient Jose Ferreira was despatched on a mission to Madrid, partly because Brigot was tired of seeing him hanging about, and partly because there was some genuine business to be done in the capital.

Sadie reported progress to her employer.

"Oh, yes, he's crazy enough about me," she said complacently, "and I'm going a little crazy myself. How long is this to go on?"

"Another week?" suggested Cartwright, smiling approvingly at the gloom on the pretty face. "Have you mentioned the fact that you've taken a fancy to his land?"

She nodded.

"He wanted to give it to me there and then," she said, "but you know what these Spaniards are. If I had accepted, there would have been nothing for me but the front door."

"Quite right," agreed Cartwright. "He is the kind of fish you must play. Did he say anything about other offers he had received for the property?"

The girl nodded.

"He spoke about you," she said; "he called you Benson – is that your real name?"

"It is good enough," said Cartwright.

"It is queer," mused the girl, looking at him thoughtfully, "that I never meet any of your friends in Paris, and that nobody knows you – by name. I went down to your flat on the Avenue of the Grand Army," she confessed frankly, "and asked the concierge. You're Benson there too."

Cartwright chuckled.

"In my business," he said, "it is necessary that one should be discreet. The name which goes in London is not good enough for Paris. And vice versa," he added.

"You're a strange man. I suppose if you marry me in the name of Benson it will be legal?" she asked dubiously.

"Of course it will be legal. I'm surprised at a girl of your intelligence asking such a question," said Cartwright. "What is the programme for tonight?"

She pulled a little face.

"The Marigny and supper at Corbets – supper in a private dining-room."

He nodded.

"So it's come to that, has it? Well, you ought to make good tonight, Sadie. Remember, I am willing to pay up to fifty thousand pounds. It is going to be a tough job raising that money, and it will break my heart to pay it. But it will not only break my heart, but it will break me everlastingly and confoundedly to pay the man's own price – and his property must be bought."

"I'll do my best," said the girl, "but you have no doubt in your mind that it is going to be hard."

He nodded.

At one o'clock the next morning he sat reading in his room, when a knock came to his door and the girl came in. She was half hysterical, but the light of triumph was in her eyes.

"Got it," she said.

"Got it!" he repeated in wonder. "You don't mean he sold?"

She nodded.

"For ten thousand pounds – three hundred thousand francs. What do you think of your little Sadie?"

"Are you serious?" he asked.

She nodded, smiling.

"What did he – ?" he began.

She hesitated and closed her eyes.

"Don't talk about it," she said quickly. "I have to see him tomorrow at his lawyers, and the property will be transferred to me."

"And after?"

She smiled grimly.

"The after-part will not be as pleasant as M. Brigot imagines," she said. "I tell you, that fellow's crazy – stark, staring mad. But I felt an awful beast, and I think he'll kill me when he discovers I've sold him."

"Don't let that worry you," said Cartwright easily.

5

He saw the girl down to her waiting auto, and went back to his rooms to think. It was curious that at that hour, when the big trouble on his mind seemed likely to roll away, that his thoughts flew instantly to Maxell. What would the prim Maxell say, if he knew? He was satisfied that Maxell would not only disapprove, but would instantly and without notice sever all connection with the adventurous company promoter. Maxell would be outraged, appalled. Cartwright smiled at the thought.

He was under no illusion as to his own conduct. He knew he was acting despicably; but this view he dismissed from his mind as being too unpleasant for contemplation. Maxell was a prig – a necessary prig, but none the less priggish. He was necessary, at any rate, to Cartwright. Anyway, Maxell stood to win if the scheme went through.

Cartwright had reached nearly the end of his financial tether, and his whole future was bound up in the success or failure of the new promotion. He had exhausted every bit of his credit in order to take up the Angera property which he knew was rich in gold, and offered possibilities which no project of his had offered before.

He had milked his other companies dry, he had played with reserves; all except his Anglo-Parisian Finance Company, where the directors were too strong to allow him his own way; and, although Maxell was not aware of the fact, his "partner" had spent fabulous sums, not only in acquiring the land itself but in purchasing other gold-mining property in the region. It was a gamble, and a dangerous gamble. He was risking the substance of his fortune for the shadow of unlimited wealth.

Yet, was it a risk? he asked himself; with the properties that he could include in his new North Morocco Gold-Mining Association – that was to be the title of the new company – there could be no doubt as to the result of the public issue. The British public dearly love a gamble, and a gold-mining gamble, with all its mysteries and uncertainties, more dearly than any.

He went to bed late, but was taking his chocolate and roll before a little café on the boulevard before nine. At half-past nine he was joined by the girl.

Cartwright had been undecided as to whether he should take his *petit déjeuner* outside or inside the café, and had decided, since the morning was bright and warm, to breakfast under the striped awning in full view of the street. Such great events hang upon slight issues.

Scarcely had the girl seated herself opposite to him, when a pedestrian, passing on the other side of the boulevard, halted and stared. Mr Ferreira had sharp eyes and a wit not altogether dulled by his monotonous occupation.

Cartwright produced a bulky package from his pocket and laid it on the table before the girl.

"Put that in your bag and be careful with it," he said; "there are three hundred thousand francs in notes. When the property is transferred to you, you must bring the transfer along to me."

"What about your promise?" she asked suspiciously.

"That I will keep," he said. "Don't forget that you have the best guarantee in the possession of the transfer. Legally, it is your property until it is made over to me."

She sat looking at the package absently, and presently she said: "You've got to get me out of Paris at once. Otherwise I am due to leave by the Sud Express – with Brigot."

He nodded.

"There is a train for Harve at two-fifteen," he said.

He saw her into her car – another indiscretion since it brought him out of the shadow which the awning afforded, and gave the observer on the other side of the road an unmistakable view.

Brigot was waiting for her – a heavy-eyed, weary-looking man, whose hand shook whenever it rose to stroke his short, pointed beard.

His lawyer watched him curiously as he stepped forward to meet the girl with hands outstretched. It was not the first time that he had seen his client overwhelmed by a pretty face.

"Everything is ready, Nanette," said the eager M. Brigot. ("Nanette" was the new-found name which Sadie O'Grady employed for this adventure.) "See here, I have all the documents ready!"

"And I have the money," smiled the girl as she put the package down on the table.

"The money!" Señor Brigot waved such sordid matters out of existence with a magnificent flourish. "What is money?"

"Count it," said the girl.

"I will do no such thing," said the other extravagantly. "As a caballero, it hurts me to discuss money in connection – "

But his lawyer had no sentiment, and had slipped the string from the package and was now busily counting the thousand-franc notes. When he had finished, he put them on the desk.

"Can I see you one moment, M. Brigot?" he asked.

Brigot, holding the girl's hand and devouring her with his eyes, turned impatiently.

"No, no," he said. "The document, my friend, the document! Give me a pen!"

"There is one point in the deed I must discuss," said the lawyer firmly, "if mademoiselle will excuse us for a moment – " He opened the door of his inner office invitingly and with a shrug M. Brigot followed him in.

"I have told you, monsieur," said the lawyer, "that I do not think your action is wise. You are surrendering a property for a sum less than a quarter of what you paid for it to a perfectly unknown woman – "

"M. l'Avocat," said the other gravely, "you are speaking of a lady who to me is more precious than life!"

The lawyer concealed a smile.

"I have often spoken to you about ladies who have been more precious to you than life," he said dryly, "but in their cases, no transfer of valuable property was involved. What do you know of this lady?"

"I know nothing except that she is adorable," said the reckless Spaniard. "But for the fact that, alas! my wife most obstinately refuses to die or divorce me, I should be honoured to make madame my wife. As it is, what a pleasure to give her the land on which to build a beautiful villa overlooking my gorgeous Tangier – I am moving to Tangier very soon to look after my other property – and to know that her blessed presence – "

The lawyer spread out despairing hands.

"Then there is nothing to be done," he said. "I only tell you that you are transferring a valuable property to a lady who is comparatively unknown to you, and it seems to me a very indiscreet and reckless thing to do."

They returned again to the outer apartment, where the girl had been standing nervously twisting the moiré bag in her hand.

"Here is the document, madame," said the lawyer to her relief. "Señor Brigot will sign here" – he indicated a line – "and you will sign there. I will cause these signatures to be witnessed, and a copy of the document will be forwarded for registration."

The girl sat down at the table, and her hand shook as she took up the pen. It was at that moment that Jose Ferreira dashed into the room.

He stood open-mouthed at the sight of the girl at the table. He tried to speak, but the sound died in his throat. Then he strode forward, under the glaring eye of his employer.

"This woman – this woman!" he gasped.

"Ferreira," cried Brigot in a terrible voice, "you are speaking of a lady who is my friend!"

"She – she" – the man pointed to her with shaking finger – "she is the woman! She escaped!… The woman I told you of, who ran away with an Englishman from Tangier!"

Brigot stared from one to the other.

"You're mad," he said.

"She is the woman," squeaked Ferreira, "and the man also is in Paris. I saw them together this morning at the Café Furnos! The man who was in Tangier, of whom I told the señor, and this woman, Sadie O'Grady!"

Brigot looked at the girl. She had been caught off her guard, and never once had the keen eyes of the lawyer left her. Given some warning, she might have dissembled and carried the matter through with a high hand. But the suddenness of the accusation, the amazingly unexpected vision of Jose, had thrown her off her guard, and Brigot did not need to look twice at her to know that the charges of his subordinate were justified. She was not a born conspirator, nor was she used to intrigues of this character.

Brigot gripped her by the arm and pulled her from the chair. He was half mad with rage and humiliation.

"What is the name of this man?" he hissed. "The name of the man who took you from Tangier and brought you here?"

She was white as death and terribly afraid.

"Benson," she stammered.

"Benson!"

The lawyer and Brigot uttered the words together, and the Spaniard, releasing his hold, stepped back.

"So it was Benson!" he said softly. "Our wonderful Englishman who wanted to swindle me out of my property, eh? And I suppose he sent you, my beautiful American widow, to purchase land for your villa! Now, you can go back to Mr Benson and tell him that, if my property is good enough for him to buy, it is good enough for me to keep. You – you!"

He made a dart at her with upraised hand, but the lawyer was before him and gently pushed him back.

He jerked his head to the girl and, shaking like a leaf, she stepped to the door and went stumbling down the stairs, which she had mounted with such confidence a few minutes before.

Cartwright received the news with extraordinary equanimity.

"It has saved us the bother of going out of Paris," he said thoughtfully. "And it was my own fault. I never connected that infernal fellow Ferreira with Brigot's enterprises. And anyway, we should not have met in public. He said he saw us at the café, did he?"

The girl nodded.

"I did my best," she faltered.

"Of course you did your best," said Cartwright, patting her hand. "it is tough luck, but it can't be helped."

There was a long silence, then:

"What about me?" asked the girl. "Where do I come in? I suppose you have no further use for my services?"

Cartwright smiled.

"Of course I have," he said genially. Then, after a longer pause, "Do you know that you're the only person in this world that I have ever taken so completely into my confidence and shown what, for a better expression, I will call the seamy side of my business? I'd like to tell you a lot more, because it would be a relief to me to get it off my chest. But I'm telling you this, that if I marry you today, you'll have to play your part to save me from everlasting ruin."

"Ruin?" she said, startled, and he laughed.

"Not the kind of ruin that means you'll go short of food," he said, "but the sort of ruin that may mean – well, ruin from my point of view. Now you must understand this thing clearly, Sadie. I'm out for a big stake, and if I don't pull it off, it's as likely as not that I'll go out. You're a clever, useful sort of kid, and I have an idea that you may be even more useful. But there's to be no sentiment in this marriage, mind! You have just to sit here and hold tight and do as you're told, and you haven't got to pry into my business any further than I want you to. And if I go away and don't come back, you must reckon me as dead. I've a lot of business in America and elsewhere, which often takes me away for months at a time, and you're not to get uneasy. But if you don't hear from me – why, you can go down to the Lafayette and buy yourself the grandest little suit of mourning that you can afford!"

"Shall I be able to afford it?" she asked.

He nodded.

"I shall put some *Rentes* to your credit at the Lyonnais. That will give you a steady income in case anything happens."

The girl was troubled.

"I don't quite like this idea," she said. "What will happen?"

Mr Cartwright flicked away the ash from the end of his cigar and said cheerfully:

"That depends entirely upon the view which is taken of a certain prospectus issued in London this morning."

6

The New Angera Syndicate was registered as a private company, and its prospectus was not made public. Officially, the shares were not offered to general subscription, and actually they had been subscribed – or the first issue of five hundred thousand had – by a little group of shrewd speculators in the City of London, who, before now, had made vast sums from Cartwright's promotions. The five hundred thousand shares brought in about half that number of pounds, and nobody doubted that the properties consolidated for the purposes of flotation included the block of claims described in the prospectus as "lately the property of Señor Brigot."

Gold had been found on the Angera reef, and gold in sufficient quantity to make the new company a very promising speculation. That Brigot's property could be made to pay, had it been properly managed, was common knowledge in the City of London. A dozen offers had been made for this concession, but none had been quite acceptable to Señor Brigot, whose estimate of the value of the mine varied with the passing hour.

Probably, had it been possible to secure an interview with M. Brigot at one o'clock in the afternoon, when he arose with a splitting head and a dry throat, his possessions might have been acquired at the price of a quart of sweet champagne.

But, as the day progressed and his views of life became more charitable, his estimate expanded until, by seven o'clock in the evening, which hour he as a rule reserved for any business discussion, his figure was awe-inspiring. Nobody in the City doubted for one moment that Cartwright had purchased the property. Though his system of finance might not commend itself to the barons and even the baronets of Capel Court, there was no question of his honesty.

Was it by some extraordinary fluke that Maxell, who had hitherto shared in the profits of promotion, had kept aloof from this last and greatest of Cartwright's flutters? No application for shares was ever found. He heard (he said at a subsequent inquiry) in a roundabout way of the flotation, and saw a copy of the prospectus, and was a little worried. He knew that when he had left Cartwright in Paris, not only was the Brigot mine outside of his friend's control, but there was precious little prospect of bringing the Spaniard to a reasonable frame of mind.

Cartwright must have done his work quickly, he thought, and have paid heavily; and this latter reflection worried him even more because he had a fairly accurate idea as to the condition of Cartwright's private finances. His private thoughts on this occasion are set forth in the report of the Attorney-General's Committee of Investigation.

He was eating his solitary dinner in Cavendish Square when the telephone bell rang and the voice of Sir Gregory Fane, the Attorney-General, saluted him.

"I should like to see you, Maxell," he said. "Will you come round to Clarges Street after dinner?"

"Certainly," replied Maxell promptly, and hung up the receiver, wondering what new difficulties had arisen, which called for a consultation; for he was not on visiting terms with Mr Attorney.

In the tiny drawing-room of the house occupied by the Cabinet Minister, Maxell was surprised to find another visitor waiting – no less a person than Fenshaw, the Prime Minister's private secretary.

The Attorney-General came straight to the point.

"Maxell," he said, "we want your seat in the House of Commons."

"The deuce you do!" said Maxell, raising his eyebrows.

The Attorney nodded.

"We also want to give you some reward for the excellent services you have rendered to the Government," he said. "But mostly" – his eyes twinkled – "it is necessary to find a seat for Sir Milton Boyd –

the Minister of Education has been defeated at a by-election, as you know."

The other nodded. The communication was a surprise to him and he wondered exactly what position was to be offered him which would involve his resignation from the House. For one brief, panicky moment he had connected Cartwright and his delinquencies with this request for an interview, but the Attorney's speech had dispelled that momentary fear.

"Quilland, as you know, has been raised to the Court of Appeal," said the Attorney, speaking of a well-known Chancery Judge, "and we are departing from our usual practice by bringing over a man from the King's Bench to take his place. Now, Maxell, how does a judgeship appeal to you?"

The KC could only stare.

Of the many things he did not expect, it was elevation to the Bench, although he was a sound, good lawyer, and the Bench is the ambition of every silk.

"I would like that," he said huskily.

"Good!" said the brisk Attorney. "Then we will regard it as settled. The appointment will not be announced for two or three days, so you've a chance of clearing up your more urgent work and preparing a letter for your constituents. You might say a kind word for the new candidate who isn't particularly popular in your part of the world."

One of Maxell's first acts was to write a letter to Cartwright. All Cartwright's correspondence went to his London office, and was forwarded under separate cover to Paris. It was a long letter, recapitulating their friendly relationship, and ending:

> This promotion, of course, means that we can no longer be associated in business, and I have instructed my broker to sell all the shares I possess in your and other companies forthwith. As you know, I have very definite views about the high prestige of the Bench; and whilst, in any circumstances, I feel that I can go to that dignified position with clean hands, my mind will be

freer if I cut all the cords which hold me to commerce of every shape and description.

Three days later the letter came to Cartwright, and he read it through with a thoughtful expression on his face. He read it twice before he slowly folded it and put it into his inside pocket.

Maxell was to be made a Judge!

He had never considered that contingency, and did not know whether to be pleased or sorry. He was losing the service of a man who had been a directing force in his life, greater than Maxell himself ever imagined. It was not so much the advice which he asked and received from the King's Counsel, but rather Cartwright had secured help by the simple process of making a study of the other's moods and expressions.

He knew the half-frown which greeted some schemes, put forward tentatively over the dinner table, and it was that little sign of displeasure which could squash the scheme rather than any considered advice which Maxell might have given. He was losing a good advocate, a very sound legal adviser. He shrugged his shoulders. Well, it did not matter very much. Fate had put a period to an old phase of life, and many things had come to an end coincidently. He was taking his afternoon tea when the letter had arrived, and the new Mrs Cartwright marked with interest the depression which followed the arrival of the mail.

The new period was beginning excitingly, he thought. He had found a new method of doing business, bolder and more desperate than any he had attempted before; and with this development he had lost a man upon whom he placed a great deal of reliance. Incidentally, he had just been married, but this fact did not bulk very largely in his reckoning. Maxell might serve him yet. The memory of an old business partnership – for in such an aspect did Cartwright interpret their previous relationship – the memory, too, of favours done, of financial dangers shared, might serve him well if things went wrong. Maxell had a pull with the Government – a greater pull, since he was now a Judge of the Supreme Court.

Maxell a Judge! It seemed queer. Cartwright had all the properly constituted Englishman's reverence for the Bench. In spite of much experience in litigation, and an acquaintance with lawyers of all kinds and stations, he reserved his awe for the god-like creature who sat in wig and gown, and dispensed justice even-handedly.

"Have you had a worrying letter?" asked the girl.

He shook his head

"No, no," he said, a little impatiently; "it is nothing."

She had hoped for a glimpse of the envelope, but was disappointed. Curiously enough, she ascribed the fact that her husband passed under a strange name and would not divulge his own, to a cause which was far from the truth, and was a great injustice to a man who, if he had not given her his proper name, had given her a title to whatever name he had. That thought she revealed for the first time.

"Do you know what I think?" she said unexpectedly.

"I didn't know you thought very much," he smiled. "In what particular department of speculation does your mind wander?"

"Don't be sarcastic," she answered. She was a little afraid of sarcasm, as are all children and immature grown-ups. "It was about your name I was thinking."

He frowned.

"Why the dickens don't you leave my name alone?" he snapped. "I have told you that it is all for your good that I'm called Benson and known as Benson in this town. When we go to London you will discover my name."

She nodded.

"I know why you keep it dark."

He looked at her sharply.

"Why do I keep it dark?" he asked, fixing his eyes on her.

"Because you're married already."

He looked at her for a moment, and then burst into such a peal of laughter that the girl knew her shot was wide of the mark.

"You're a weird person," he said, getting up. "I'm going out to see an old friend of ours."

"Of ours?" she asked suspiciously.

"Brigot is the gentleman's name."

"He won't see you," she said decidedly.

"Oh, won't he?" said the grim man. "I rather think he will."

M. Brigot would not willingly have received one whose name was anathema, but Cartwright got over the difficulty of his reception by the simple process of sending up a card inscribed with the name of Brigot's lawyer.

"You!" spluttered M. Brigot, rising to his feet as the other entered the room and closed the door behind him. "This is an outrage! It is monstrous! You will leave this house immediately, or I will send for the police!"

"Now, just keep quiet for a moment, Brigot," said Cartwright, seating himself coolly. "I have come to see you as one business man to another."

"I refuse to discuss any business with you," stormed his unwilling host. "You are a scoundrel, a conspirator – bah! why do I talk to you?"

"Because you're broke!" said Cartwright in calm, level tones, and he used the Spanish word for "broke," which is so much more expressive than any word in English.

The conversation was carried on in this language, for Cartwright had an intimate knowledge of its idioms and even of its patois.

"Your creditors in Paris are gathering round like hawks about a dead cow. Your attempt to sell your Moorish property has been a failure."

"You know a great deal," sneered Brigot. "Possibly you also know that I am going to work the mine myself."

The Englishman chuckled.

"I've heard that said of you for years," said he, "but the truth is, you're wholly incapable of working anything. You're one of nature's little spenders – now, Brigot, don't let us quarrel. There is a time to end feuds like ours, and this is that time. I am a business man, and so are you. You're as anxious to sell your property at a good price as I am to buy it. I've come to make you an offer."

M. Brigot laughed sarcastically.

"Ten thousand pounds?" he demanded with gentle irony. "To build a house for a beautiful American widow, eh?"

Cartwright accepted the gibe with a smile.

"I'm not going to show you my hand," he said.

"It will be infamously dirty," said M. Brigot, who was in his bright six o'clock mood.

"I know there is gold in the Angera," the other went on, without troubling to notice the interruption, "and I know that, properly worked, your mine may pay big profits."

"I will sell out," said M. Brigot after consideration, "but at a price. I have told you before I will sell out – at a price."

"But what a price!" said Cartwright, raising his eyebrows and with a gesture of extravagant despair. "It is all the money in the world!"

"Nevertheless, it is the price," said M. Brigot comfortably.

"I'll tell you what I am willing to do." Cartwright stroked his chin as though the solution had just occurred to him. "I will float your property in London, tacking on a number of other properties which I have bought in the neighbourhood. I am willing to pay you two hundred thousand pounds – that is to say, six million francs."

M. Brigot was interested. He was so interested that, for the moment, he could forget his animosity and private grievances. It was true that, as Cartwright had said, his creditors were becoming noisy.

"In cash, of course?" he said suddenly.

Cartwright shook his head.

"You can have a portion in cash and the rest in shares."

"Bah!" Brigot snapped his fingers. "I also can issue shares, my friend. What are shares? Pieces of paper which are not worth their ink. No, no, you deceive me. I thought you had come to me with a genuine offer. There is no business to be done between you and me, Mr Cartwright. Good evening."

Cartwright did not move.

"A portion in cash – say, fifteen thousand pounds," he suggested; "that is a lot of money."

"To you – yes, but not to me," said the magnificent Brigot. "Give me two-thirds in cash and I will take the rest in shares. That is my last word."

Cartwright rose.

"This offer is open until – when?"

"Until tomorrow at this hour," replied Brigot.

As Cartwright was going, a man tapped at the door. It was Brigot's "secretary," who was also his valet. He handed a telegram to the Spaniard, and Brigot opened and read. He was a long time digesting its contents, and Cartwright waited for a favourable opportunity to say goodbye. All the time his mind was working, and he thought he saw daylight. Two-thirds of the money could be raised, and he could breathe again.

Presently Brigot folded up the telegram and put it in his pocket, and there was on his face a beatific smile.

"Good night, Señor Brigot," said Cartwright. "I will see you tomorrow with the money."

"It will have to be big money, my friend," said Brigot, and there was a note of exultation in his voice. "To buy my little property will cost you half a million English pounds."

Cartwright gasped.

"What do you mean?" he demanded quickly.

"Do you know Solomon Brothers, the financiers of London?"

"I know them very well," replied Cartwright steadily. He had good reason to know Solomon Brothers, who had taken a large block of shares in his new syndicate.

"I have just had a telegram from Solomon Brothers," said Señor Brigot, speaking slowly, "and they ask me to give them the date when my property was transferred to your syndicate. They tell me it is included in your properties which you have floated. You know best, Mr Cartwright, whether my little mine is worth half a million English pounds to you – especially if I put a date agreeable to you."

"Blackmail, eh?" said Cartwright between his teeth, and without a word left the room.

7

He went straight back to his flat on the Avenue of the Grand Army, and the girl could see by his face that something had happened.

"You might pack my bag, will you?" he said almost brusquely. "I have a letter or two to write. I'm going to London. Important business has arisen, and I may be gone some time."

Wisely she asked no questions, but carried out his instructions. When she came back from the room with a little gripsack packed, he was blotting the envelope of the last letter.

"Post these after I have gone," he said.

"Shall I come down to the station and see you off?"

He shook his head.

"The less you and I are seen together, the better, I think," he said with a faint smile.

He opened a drawer of his desk and took out a cash-box. From this he extracted a thick wad of notes, and, counting them rapidly, he tossed a respectable bundle into her lap.

"You may want this," he said. "You know you have a regular income, but you must keep in touch with the Lyonnais. For the moment I should advise you to go to" – he looked at the ceiling for inspiration – "to Nice or Monte Carlo. Keep away from the tables," he added humorously.

"But – but," said the bewildered girl, "for how long will you be gone? Can't I come with you?"

"That is impossible," he said sharply. "You must go to the South of France, leave by tonight's train. Give your address to nobody, and take another name if necessary."

"Are things very wrong?"

"Pretty bad," he said. "But don't worry. I may be gone for a year, even more. There are plenty of things you can do, but don't go back into the profession yet awhile."

"I thought of taking up cinema work," she said.

He nodded.

"You might do worse than go to America – if I am a long time gone."

He stuffed the remainder of the notes into his pocket, picked up his bag, and with no other farewell than a curt nod, left her.

She was only to see him once again in her lifetime.

He crossed the Channel by the night boat and came to London in the early hours of the morning. He drove straight away to his hotel, had a bath and shaved. His plan was fairly well formed. Everything depended upon the charity which Messrs Solomon Brothers might display towards his strange lapse.

At breakfast he read in *The Times* that "Mr Justice Maxell took his seat upon the Bench" on the previous day, and that paragraph, for some reason, seemed to cheer him.

At ten o'clock he was in the City. At half past ten he was interviewing the senior partner of Solomon Brothers, a man with an expressionless face, who listened courteously to the somewhat lame excuses which Cartwright offered.

"It was a mistake of a blundering clerk," said Cartwright airily. "As soon as I discovered the error, I came back to London to withdraw all the money which had been subscribed."

"It is a pity you didn't come back yesterday, Mr Cartwright," said Solomon.

"What do you mean?"

"I mean," said the other, "that we have already placed this matter in the hands of our solicitors. I suggest that you had better interview them."

Cartwright made a further pilgrimage to the solicitors of Solomon Brothers, and found them most unwilling to see him. That was an ominous sign, and he went back to his office in Victoria Street conscious that a crisis was at hand. At any rate, the girl was out of the way; but, what was more important, she, one of the principal witnesses in so far as Brigot and his property were concerned, was not available for those who might bring a charge against him. She was his wife, and her lips were sealed, and this consequence of his marriage was one which he had not wholly overlooked when he had contracted his strange alliance.

What a fool he had been! The property might have been transferred and in his hands, if he had not antagonised a wretched little Spanish theatrical manager. But, he reflected, if he had not antagonised that manager, he would not have possessed the instrument for extracting the transfer from the amorous Brigot.

At the top of a heap of letters awaiting him was one written in a firm boyish hand, and Cartwright made a little grimace, as though for the first time recognising his responsibility.

"Take A Chance Anderson; my lad, you will have to take a chance," he said, and pushed the letter aside unopened.

He lunched at his club, sent a brief letter to Maxell, and returned to his office at two in the afternoon. His clerk told him that a man was waiting for him in the inner office. Cartwright hesitated with his hand on the door; then, setting his teeth, he stepped in.

The stranger rose.

"Are you Mr Alfred Cartwright?" he asked.

"That is my name," replied Cartwright.

"I am Inspector Guilbury, of the City Police," said the stranger, "and I shall take you into custody on charges under the Companies Act, and a further charge of conspiracy to defraud."

Cartwright laughed.

"Go ahead," he said.

All the week preceding the trial, Cartwright's heart was filled with warm gratitude to his erstwhile friend. He did not doubt, when his solicitor told him that Mr Justice Maxell would try his case, that Maxell had gone a long way out of his way to get himself appointed the Old Bailey judge. How like Maxell it was – that queer, solemn stick – and how loyal!

Cartwright had a feeling for Maxell which he had never had before. At first he had feared the embarrassment which might be Maxell's at having to try a case in which an old friend was implicated, and had even hoped that the new judge would have nothing to do with the trial. He did not despair of Maxell pulling strings on his behalf, and he realised that much could be done by judicious lobbying.

The charge against him was a grave one. He had not realised how serious it was until he had seen that respectful array of counsel in the Lord Mayor's Court, and had heard his misdemeanours reduced to cold legal phraseology. But he did not wholly despair. Brigot had been coming to London to give evidence, and on his journey there had occurred an incident which suggested to the accused man that Providence was fighting on his side. The Spaniard had had a stroke in the train to Calais, and the doctors reported that he might not recover. Not that Brigot's evidence was indispensable. There was, apparently, a letter and two telegrams in existence, in the course of which Brigot denied that he had ever parted with his property; and the onus lay upon Cartwright to prove that he had acted in a bona fide manner – that was impossible of proof, and nobody knew this better than Cartwright.

And ever his mind reverted to the singular act of generosity on the part of his old friend. He did not doubt for one moment that Maxell had "worked" the case so that it fell to him to try it.

It was a bright morning in May when he came up the steps of the Old Bailey and took his place in the dock. Almost immediately after, the Judge and the Sheriff entered from the door behind the plain oaken bench. How well the judicial robes became Maxell, thought Cartwright. He bowed slightly and received as slight a bow in reply. Maxell was looking pale. His face was drawn, and there was resolution in his speech and in his eyes.

"Before this case proceeds," he said, "I wish to direct attention to a statement in one of the newspapers this morning, that I was associated with the accused in business, and that I am in some way involved, directly or indirectly, in the company promotion – either as a shareholder or an indirect promoter – which is the subject of the present charge. I wish to utter an emphatic denial to that statement."

He spoke clearly and slowly and looked the prisoner straight in the eye, and Cartwright nodded.

"I can only endorse your lordship's statement," he said emphatically. "Your lordship has never had any dealings with me or any business transactions whatsoever."

It was a minor sensation which provided a headline for the evening newspapers. The case proceeded. It was not particularly involved and the witnesses were few but vital. There were those business men who had subscribed or promised to subscribe to the syndicate. There was Mr Solomon, who could give an account of his dealings with the prisoner. But, most damning of all, was a sworn statement made by Brigot before an English solicitor, a Commissioner of Oaths. And it was such a statement which only documentary proof, produced by the accused man, could refute.

Cartwright listened to the evidence untroubled of mind. He knew that his counsel's speech, delivered with such force, was little less than an admission of guilt and a plea for mercy. The last word would be with the Judge. A verdict of "guilty" there must necessarily be. But he thought that, when later his counsel pleaded for a minimum sentence, he saw a responsive look in the Judge's eyes.

The stigma of imprisonment did not greatly distress Cartwright. He had lived on the narrow border-line of illegalities too long; he had weighed chances and penalties too nicely to bother about such ephemeral things as "honour." His system of finance was reviewed, and certain minor charges arising out of the manipulation of funds were gone into. It was late in the evening when the Judge began his summing up.

It was a fair, if a conventional address he delivered to the jury. Obviously, thought Cartwright, he could do nothing less than call attention to the serious nature of the charge, the interests involved, the betrayal of shareholders, and the like. On the whole, the summing up did not diminish the comforting sense that the worst that lay before him was a few months' imprisonment and then a start in another land under another name. He never doubted his ability to make money. The summing up was ended, and the jury retired. They were gone twenty minutes, and when they came back it was a foregone conclusion what their verdict would be.

"Do you find the prisoner at the bar guilty or not guilty?"

"Guilty," was the reply.

"And is that the verdict of you all?"

"It is."

Justice Maxell was examining his notes, and presently he closed the little book which he was consulting.

"The charge against Alfred Cartwright," he said, "is one of the most serious which could be brought against a business man. The jury have returned a verdict of guilty, and I must say that I concur in that verdict. I am here in my place" – his voice shook a little – "to administer and maintain the laws of England. I must do all that in me is possible to preserve the purity of commercial life and the condition of English commercial honesty."

Cartwright waited for that "but" – it did not come.

"In view of the seriousness of the frauds and irregularities which the accused has committed, with a cynical disregard for the happiness or fortune of those people whose interests should have been his own, I cannot do less than pass a sentence which will serve as an example to all wrongdoers."

Cartwright gasped and gripped the edge of the dock.

"You, Alfred Cartwright," said Maxell, and again looked him straight in the eye, "will be kept in penal servitude for twenty years."

Cartwright swallowed something. Then he leaned across the edge of the dock.

"You swine!" he said huskily, and then the warders dragged him away.

Two days later there was a new sensation. The newspapers announced that Mr Justice Maxell had been compelled, on account of ill-health, to resign from the Bench, and that His Majesty had been pleased to confer a baronetcy of the United Kingdom upon the ex-Judge.

8

Some nine years after the events detailed in the last chapter, a fairly clever young actress who had drifted into the cinematograph business, faced one of the many disappointments which had made up her life. In many ways the disappointment was more bitter than any she had previously experienced, because she had banked so heavily upon success.

If there was any satisfaction to be had out of the new tragedy it was to be found in the fact that the fault was not entirely hers. An impartial critic might, indeed, absolve her from all responsibility.

In this particular instance she regarded herself in the light of a martyr to indifferent literature – not without reason.

When the Westminster Art Film Company was tottering on its last legs, Mr Willie Ellsberger, chairman and chief victim, decided on one big throw for fortune. The play decided upon does not matter, because it was written by Willie himself, with the assistance of his advertising man, but it contained all the stunts that had ever got by in all the photo plays that had ever been produced, and in and out of every breathless situation flashed Sadie O'Grady, the most amazing, the most charming, the most romantic, the highest salaried artiste that filmland had ever known.

Sadie O'Grady had come to London from Honolulu, after she had inherited her father's considerable fortune. She came, a curious visitor, to the studios, merely as a spectator, and had laughingly refused Mr Ellsberger's first offer, that gentleman having been attracted by her perfect face and the grace of her movements; but at last, after extraordinary persuasion, she had agreed to star in that stupendous production, "The Soul of Babylon," for a fee of £25,000, which was to be distributed amongst certain Honolulu charities in which she was interested.

"No," she told a newspaper man, "this is to be my first and my last film. I enjoy the work very much, but naturally it takes up a great deal of my time."

"Are you returning to Honolulu?" asked our representative.

"No," replied Miss O'Grady, "I am going on to Paris. My agent has bought me the Duc de Montpelier's house in the Avenue d'Etoile."

A week after the picture was finished, Miss Sadie O'Grady waited on the chairman by appointment.

"Well, Sadie," said that gentleman, leaning back in his chair, and smiling unhappily, "it's a flivver!"

"You don't say!" said Sadie aghast.

"We ran it off for the big renter from the North, and he says it is about as bad as it can be, and that all the good in it is so obviously stolen, that he dare not risk the injunction which would follow the first exhibition. Did Simmonds pay you your last week's salary?"

"No, Mr Ellsberger," said the girl.

Ellsberger shrugged.

"That sets me back another twenty pounds," he said and reached for his cheque-book. "It is tough on you, Sadie, but it's tougher on us. I'm not so sure that it is so tough on you, though. I spent a fortune advertising you. There isn't anybody in this country who hasn't heard of Sadie O'Grady, and," he added grimly, "you've more publicity than I hope I shall get when this business goes into the hands of the Official Receiver."

"So there's no more work?" asked the girl after a pause.

Mr Ellsberger's hands said: "What can I do?"

"You ought not to have any difficulty in getting a shop," he said, "with your figure."

"Especially when the figure's twenty pounds a week," she said unsmilingly. "I was a fool ever to leave Paris. I was doing well there and I wish I'd never heard of the cinema business."

Still young and pretty and slim, with a straight nose and a straighter mouth, she had no appeal for Mr Ellsberger, who in matters of business had an unsympathetic nature.

"Why don't you go back to Paris?" he said, speaking very deliberately and looking out of the window. "Perhaps that affair has blown over by now."

"What affair?" she asked sharply. "What do you mean?"

"I've friends in Paris," said the chairman, "good, bright boys who go around a lot, and they know most of what's going on in town."

She looked at him, biting her lips thoughtfully.

"Reggie van Rhyn – that's the trouble you heard about?"

Mr Ellsberger nodded.

"I didn't know what happened, and I'll never believe in a thousand years that I stabbed him," she said vigorously. "I've always been too much of a lady for that sort of thing – I was educated at a convent."

Mr Ellsberger yawned.

"Take that to Curtis, will you," he said. "If he can get any free publicity for you, why, I'll be glad. Now take my advice – stay on. I've put Sadie O'Grady way up amongst the well-known products of Movieland, and you'll be a fool if you quit just when the public is getting interested in you. I'm in bad, but that doesn't affect you, Sadie, and there ain't a producer in England who wouldn't jump at you and give you twice the salary I'm paying."

She stood up, undecided. Ellsberger was growing weary of the interview. He made a great show of pulling out notepaper and rang the bell for his stenographer.

"The publicity's fine," she admitted, "and I've felt good about the work. Why, the letters that I've had from people asking for my autograph and pictures of my Honolulu estate" – she smiled a little frostily – "people in society, too. Why, a titled man who wrote to me from Bournemouth, Sir John Maxell – "

"Sir John Maxell!"

Mr Ellsberger was interested, indeed, he was fascinated. He waved away his stenographer.

"Sit down, Sadie," he said. "You're sure it was Maxell? Sir John Maxell?"

She nodded.

"That's him," she said. "There's class there."

"And there's money, too," said the practical Ellsberger. "Why don't you get in touch with him, Sadie? A fellow like that would think nothing of putting ten thousand into a picture if he was interested in a girl. If you happen to be the girl, Sadie, there'll be a thousand pound contract for you right away."

Her straight lips were a trifle hard.

"What you want is an angel, and the Judge is the best kind of angel you could wish for."

"Has he got money?" she asked.

"Money!" said the hands of Ellsberger. "What a ridiculous question to ask!"

"Money!" he scoffed. "Money to burn. Do you mean to say you've never heard of Sir John Maxell, never heard of the man who sent his best friend to gaol for twenty years? Why, it was the biggest sensation of the year!"

Sadie was not very interested in history, but momentarily, by virtue of the very warm and well punctuated letter which reposed in her bag, she was interested in Sir John.

"Is he married?" asked the girl naturally.

"He is not married," said Ellsberger emphatically.

"Any children?"

"There are no children, but he has a niece – he's got some legal responsibility as regards her; I remember seeing it in the newspapers, he's her guardian or something."

Mr Ellsberger looked at the girl with a speculative eye.

"Have you his letter?"

She nodded and produced the epistle.

It was polite but warm. It had some reference to her "gracious talent," to her "unexampled beauty" which had "brought pleasure to one who was no longer influenced by the commonplace," and it finished up by expressing the hope that they two would meet in the early future, and that before leaving for Paris she would honour him by being his guest for a few days.

Ellsberger handed the letter back.

"Write him," he said, "and, Sadie, consider yourself engaged for another week – write to him in my time. He's fallen for all that Press stuff, and maybe, if he's got that passionate admiration for your genius he'll – say, you don't want to stay in the picture business and finish by marrying that kind of trouble, do you?"

He pointed through the wide windows to a youth who was coming across from the studio to the office, swinging a cane vigorously.

"Observe the lavender socks and the wrist watch," he chuckled. "But don't make any mistake about Timothy Anderson. He's the toughest amateur at his weight in this or any other state and a good boy, but he's the kind of fellow that women like you marry – get acquainted with the Judge."

With only a preliminary knock, which he did not wait to hear answered, the young man had swung through the door, hat in hand.

"How do, Miss O'Grady?" he said. "I saw your picture – fine! Good acting, but a perfectly rotten play. I suppose you wrote it, Ellsberger?"

"I wrote it," admitted that gentleman gloomily.

"It bears the impression of your genius, old bird."

Timothy Anderson shook his head reproachfully.

"It only wanted you as the leading man, and it would have been dead before we put the titles in," said Ellsberger with a grin.

"I'm out of the movies for good," said Timothy Anderson, sitting himself on a table. "It is a demoralising occupation – which reminds me."

He slipped from the table, thrust his hand into his pocket, and producing a roll of notes:

"I owe you twenty-five pounds, Ellsberger," he said. "Thank you very much. You saved me from ruin and starvation."

He counted the money across, and Mr Ellsberger was undoubtedly surprised and made no attempt to conceal the fact. So surprised was he that he could be jocose.

"Fixed a big contract with Mary Pickford?" he asked.

"N-no," said Timothy, "but I struck a roulette game – and took a chance."

"Took a chance again, eh?" said Ellsberger. "One of these days you'll take a chance and never get the better of it."

"Pooh!" said the other in derision. "Do you think that's any new experience for me? Not on your life. I went into this game with just twelve pounds and my hotel bill three weeks in arrears. I was down to my last half-crown, but I played it and came out with three hundred pounds."

"Whose game was it?" asked Mr Ellsberger curiously.

"Tony Smail," and Mr Ellsberger whistled.

"Why, that's one of the toughest places in town," he said. "It is a wonder you came away with the money – and your life."

"I took a chance," said the other carelessly, and swung his legs once more over the edge of the desk. "There was some slight trouble when I came out of Smail's," he shrugged his shoulders, "just a little horseplay."

The girl had followed the conversation keenly. Any talk which circled about finance had the effect of concentrating her attention.

"Do you always take a chance?" she asked.

"Always," said the other promptly.

This woman did not appeal to him. Timothy possessed a seventh sense which he called his "Sorter," and Miss Sadie O'Grady was already sorted into the heap of folks who, had life been a veritable voyage, would have been labelled "Not Wanted."

He held out his hand to Ellsberger.

"I'm going by the next boat to New York," he said, "then I'll go to California. Maybe I'll take in Kempton on my way, for a fellow I met at the hotel has a horse running which can catch pigeons. Goodbye, Miss O'Grady. I wish you every kind of luck."

She watched him disappear, sensing his antagonism and responding thereto. If he could judge women by intuition, she judged him by reason, and she knew that here was a man whose mental attitude was one of dormant hostility.

It would be unfair to her to say that it was because she recognised the clean mind and the healthy outlook and the high principles of this young man that she disliked him. She was not wholly bad, because she had been the victim of circumstances and had lately lived a two-thousand pound life on a one-hundred pound capacity. She looked after him, biting her lips as though she were solving a great problem.

Presently she turned to Ellsberger.

"I'll write to Sir John," she said.

By a curious coincidence Timothy Anderson had the idea of approaching Sir John Maxell also, though nearly a year passed before he carried his idea into execution.

9

The initials "T A C" before young Mr Anderson's name stood for Timothy Alfred Cartwright, his pious but practical parent having, by this combination, made a bid for the protection of the saints and the patronage of Cousin Al Cartwright, reputedly a millionaire and a bachelor. It was hoped in this manner that his position on earth and in heaven would be equally secure.

What Timothy's chances are in the hereafter the reader must decide; but we do know that Cousin Al Cartwright proved both a weak reed and a whited sepulchre. Timothy's parents had departed this life two years after Alfred Cartwright had disappeared from public view, leaving behind him two years' work for a committee of Investigating Accounts.

When his surviving parent died, the boy was at school, and if he was not a prodigy of learning he was at least brilliant in parts.

Though it was with no great regret that he left school, he was old enough and shrewd enough to realise that a bowing acquaintance with the differential calculus, and the ability to conjugate the verb "avoir" did not constitute an equipment, sufficiently comprehensive (if you will forgive these long words), to meet and defeat such enemies to human progress as he was likely to meet in this cruel and unsympathetic world.

He had a small income bequeathed by his mother in a will which was almost apologetic because she left so little, and he settled himself down as a boarder in the house of a schoolmaster, and took up those branches of study which interested him, and set himself to forget other branches of education which interested him not at all.

Because of his ineradicable passion for challenging fate it was only natural that "T A C" should bear a new significance, and since some genius had christened him "Take A Chance" Anderson the name stuck. And he took chances. From every throw with fate he learnt something. He had acquired some knowledge of boxing at school, and had learnt enough of the art to enable him to head the school. Such was his faith in himself and his persuasive eloquence that he induced Sam Murphy, ex-middle-weight and proprietor of the Stag's Head, Dorking, to nominate and support him for a ten-rounds contest with that redoubtable feather-weight, Bill Schenk.

"Take A Chance" Anderson took his chance. He also took the count in the first round, and, returning to consciousness, vowed a vow – not that he would never again enter the ring, but that he would learn something more of the game before he did. Of course, it was very disgraceful that a man of his antecedents should become a professional boxer – for professional he became in the very act of failure – but that worried him not at all.

It is a matter of history that Bill Schenk was knocked out by Kid Muldoon, and that twelve months after his initiation into the prize ring "T Anderson" fought twenty rounds with the Kid and got the decision on points. Thereafter, the ring knew "Take A Chance" Anderson no more.

He took a chance on race-courses, backing horses that opened at tens and closed at twenties. He backed horses that had never won before on the assumption that they must win some time. He had sufficient money left after this adventure to buy a book of form. He devoted his undoubted talent to the study of other games of chance. He played cards for matches with a broker's clerk, who harboured secret ambitions of going to Monte Carlo with a system; he purchased on the hire system wonderfully cheap properties on the Isle of Thanet – and he worked.

For all his fooling and experimenting, for all his gambling and his chancing, Timothy never let a job of work get past him, if he could do it, and when he wasn't working for sordid lucre he was working for the good of his soul. He went to the races with a volume of Molière's plays under his arm, and between events he read, hereby acquiring the respect of the racing fraternity as an earnest student of form.

So he came by violent, yet to him easy, stages to Movieland – that Mecca which attracts all that is enterprising and romantic and restless. He took a chance in a juvenile lead, but his method and his style of actions were original. Producers are for ever on the lookout for novelty, but they put the bar up against novel styles of acting and expression. Ellsberger had tried him out because he had known his father, but more because he had won money over him when he had beaten Kid Muldoon; but even Ellsberger was compelled to suggest that Timothy put in two long years "atmosphering" before he essayed an individual role on the screen.

Timothy was not certain whether his train left at ten minutes to seven or at ten minutes past seven, so he arrived in time for the ten minutes to seven, which was characteristic of him, because he never took a chance against the inflexible systems.

He reached New York without misadventure, but on his way westward he stayed over at Nevada. He intended spending a night, but met a man with a scheme for running a mail-order business on entirely new lines, invested his money, and by some miracle managed to make it last a year. At the end of that time the police were after his partner, and Timothy was travelling eastward by easy stages.

He came back to New York with fifty-five dollars which he had won from a Westerner on the last stage of the journey. The track ran for about twenty miles along the side of the road, the wager between them was a very simple one; it was whether they would pass more men than women on the road. The Westerner chose men and Timothy chose women. For every man they saw Timothy paid a dollar, for every woman he received a dollar. In the agreed hour they passed fifty-five more women than they passed men and Timothy was that many dollars richer. There were never so many women abroad as there were that bright afternoon, and the Westerner couldn't understand it until he realised that it was Sunday – a fact which Timothy had grasped before he had made his wager.

Two months later he was back in London. How he got back he never explained. He stayed in London only long enough to fit himself up with a new kit before he presented himself at a solid mansion in Branksome Park, Bournemouth. Years and years before, Sir John Maxell had written to him, asking him to call upon him for any help he might require, and promising to assist him in whatever difficulties he might find himself. Timothy associated the offer with the death of his father – maybe they were friends.

He was shown into the sunny drawing-room bright with flowers, and he looked round approvingly. He had lived in other people's houses all his life – schools, boarding-houses, hotels and the like – and an atmosphere of home came to him like the forgotten fragrance of a garden he had known.

The servant came back.

"Sir John will see you in ten minutes, sir, but you must not keep him long, because he has to go out to meet Lady Maxell."

"Lady Maxell?" asked Timothy in surprise, "I didn't know he was married."

The servant smiled and said:

"The Judge married a year ago, sir. It was in all the newspapers."

"I don't read all the newspapers," said Timothy. "I haven't sufficient time. Who was the lady?"

The man looked round, as if fearing to be overheard.

"Sir John married the cinema lady, Miss Sadie O'Grady," he said, and the hostility in his tone was unmistakable.

Timothy gasped.

"You don't say!" he said. "Well, that beats the band! Why, I knew that da—, that lady in London!"

The servant inclined his head sideways.

"Indeed, sir," he said, and it was evident that he did not regard Timothy as being any fitter for human association by reason of his confession.

A distant bell buzzed.

"Sir John is ready, sir," he said. "I hope you will not mention the fact that I spoke of madam?"

Timothy winked, and was readmitted to the confidence of the democracy.

Sir John Maxell was standing up behind his writing table, a fine, big man with his grey hair neatly brushed back from his forehead and his blue eyes magnified behind rimless glasses.

"T A C Anderson," he said, coming round the table with slow steps. "Surely this is not the little Timothy I heard so much about years and years ago!"

"That is I, sir," said Timothy.

"Well, well," said Maxell, "I should never have known you. Sit down, my boy. You smoke, of course – everybody smokes nowadays, but it seems strange that a boy I knew in short breeches should have acquired the habit. I've heard about you," he said, as Timothy lit his cigar.

"Nothing to my discredit, I hope, sir?"

Maxell shook his head.

"I have heard about you," he repeated diplomatically, "let it go at that. Now I suppose you've come here because, five years ago, on the twenty-third of December to be correct, I wrote to you, offering to give you any help that lay in my power."

"I won't swear to the date," said Tim.

"But I will," smiled the other. "I never forget a date, I never forget a letter, I never forget the exact wording of that letter. My memory is an amazing gift. Now just tell me what I can do for you."

Timothy hesitated.

"Sir John," he said, "I have had a pretty bad time in America. I've been running in a team with a crook and I've had to pay out every cent I had in the world!"

Sir John nodded slowly.

"Then it is money you want," he said, without enthusiasm.

"Not exactly money, sir, but I'm going to try to start in London and I thought, maybe, you might give me a letter of introduction to somebody."

"Ah, well," said Maxell, brightening up, "I think I can do that for you. What did you think of doing in London?"

"I thought of getting some sort of secretarial job," he said. "Not that I know much about it!"

Sir John pinched his lower lip.

"I know a man who may help you," he said. "We were in the House of Commons together and he would give you a place in one of his offices, but unfortunately for you he has made a great deal of money and spends most of his time at Newmarket."

"Newmarket sounds good to me," said Timothy "Why, I'd take a chance there. Perhaps he'd try me out in that office?"

The Judge permitted himself to smile.

"In Newmarket," he said, "our friend does very little more, I fear, than waste his time and money on the race-course. He has half a dozen horses – I had a letter from him this morning."

He walked back to his table, searched in the litter, and presently amongst the papers pulled out a letter.

"As a matter of fact, I had some business with him and I wrote to him for information. The only thing he tells me is" – this with a gesture of despair – "that Skyball and Polly Chaw – those are the names of race-horses, I presume – will win the two big handicaps next week and that he has a flyer named Swift Kate that can beat anything – I am quoting his words – on legs over six furlongs."

He looked up over his glasses at Timothy, and on that young man's face was a seraphic smile.

"Newmarket sounds real nice to me," glowed Timothy.

Remembering the injunctions of the servant, he was taking his adieu, when his host asked, in a lower voice than that in which the conversation had been carried on:

"I suppose you have not heard from your cousin?"

Timothy looked at him in astonishment. Had Sir John asked after the Grand Llama of Tibet he would have been as well prepared to answer.

"Why, no, sir – no – er – is he alive?"

Sir John Maxell looked at him sharply.

"Alive? Of course. I thought you might have heard from him."

Timothy shook his head.

"No, sir," he said, "he disappeared. I only met him once when I was a kid. Was he a friend – er – an acquaintance of yours?"

Sir John was drumming his fingers on the desk and his mind was far away.

"Yes and no," he said shortly. "I knew him, and at one time I was friendly with him."

Suddenly he glanced at his watch, and a look of consternation came to his face.

"Great heavens!" he cried. "I promised to meet my wife a quarter of an hour ago. Goodbye! Goodbye!"

He hand-shook Timothy from the room and the young man had to find his way downstairs without guidance, because the manservant was at that moment heavily engaged.

From the floor below came a shrill, unpleasant sound, and Timothy descended to find himself in the midst of a domestic crisis. There were two ladies in the hall – one a mere silent, contained spectator, the other the principal actress. He recognised her at once, but she did not see him, because her attention was directed to the red-faced servant.

"When I ring you on the phone, I expect to be answered," she was saying. "You've nothing to do except to sit round and keep your ears open, you big, lazy devil!"

"But, my lady, I – "

"Don't answer me," she stormed. "If you think I've nothing better to do than to sit at a phone waiting till you wake up, why, you're mistaken – that's all. And if Sir John doesn't fire you – "

"Don't worry about Sir John firing me," said the man with a sudden change of manner. "I've just had about as much of you as I can stand. You keep your bossing for the movies, Lady Maxell. You're not going to try any of that stuff with me!"

She was incapable of further speech, nor was there any necessity for it since the man turned on his heels and disappeared into that mysterious region which lies at the back of every entrance hall. Then for the first time she saw Timothy.

"How do you do, Lady Maxell?"

She glared round at the interrupter, and for a moment he thought she intended venting her anger on him. She was still frowning when he took her limp hand.

"You're the Anderson boy, aren't you?" she asked a little ungraciously.

The old sense of antagonism was revived and intensified in him at the touch of her hand. She was unchanged, looking, if anything, more pretty than when he had seen her last, but the hardness at her mouth was accentuated, and she had taken on an indefinable air of superiority which differed very little from sheer insolence.

A gold-rimmed lorgnette came up to survey him, and he was nettled – only women had the power to annoy him.

"You haven't changed a bit," he bantered. "I'm sorry your eyesight is not so good as it was. Studio life is pretty tough on the eyes, isn't it?"

She closed her lorgnette with a snap, and turned to the girl.

"You'd better see what Sir John is doing," she said. "Ask him what he thinks I am, that I should wait in the hall like a tramp."

It was then that the girl came out of the shadow and Timothy saw her.

"This is the ward or niece," he said to himself, and sighed, for never had he seen a human creature who so satisfied his eye. There is a beauty which is neither statuesque nor cold, nor to be confounded with prettiness. It is a beauty which depends upon no regularity of feature or of colour, but which has its reason in its contradictions.

The smiling Madonna whom Leonardo drew had such contradictory quality as this girl possessed. For she was ninety per cent child, and carried in her face all the bubbling joy of youth. Yet she impressed Timothy as being strange and unnatural. Her meekness, her ready obedience to carry out the woman's instruction, the very dignity of her departure – these things did not fit with the character he read in her face. Had she turned curtly to this insolent woman and told her to carry her message herself, or had she flown up the stairs calling for Sir John as she went, these things would have been natural.

Lady Maxell turned upon him.

"And see here, Mr What's-your-name, if you're a friend of Sir John, you'll forget that I was ever in a studio. There are enough stories about me in Bournemouth without your adding to the collection."

"Mother's little thoroughbred!" said Timothy admiringly; "spoken like a true little lady."

In some respects he was wholly undisciplined, and had never learnt the necessity of refraining from answering back. And the woman irritated him, and irritation was a novel sensation.

Her face was dark with rage, but it was upon Sir John, descending in haste to meet his offended wife, that she turned the full batteries of her anger.

"You didn't know the time, of course. Your watch has stopped. It is hard enough for me to keep my end up without you helping to make me look foolish!"

"My dear," protested Maxell in a flurry, "I assure you – "

"You can spend your time with this sort of trash," she indicated Timothy, and Timothy bowed, "but you keep me waiting like a tailor's model at Sotheby's, of all people in the world, when you know well enough – "

"My dear," pleaded the lawyer wearily, "my watch has certainly stopped – "

"Ah! You make me tired. What are you doing with this fellow? Do you think I want reminding of movie days? Everybody knows this fellow – a cheap gambler, who's been fired out of every studio in England. You allow your servants to insult me – and now I suppose you've brought this prize-fighter to keep me in my place," and she pointed scornfully at the amused Timothy.

Half-way downstairs the girl stood watching the scene in silence, and it was only when he became conscious of her presence that Timothy began to feel a little uncomfortable.

"Well, goodbye, Sir John," he said. "I'm sorry I intruded."

"Wait," said the woman. "John, this man has insulted me! I don't know what he's come for, but I suppose he wants something. He's one of those shifty fellows that hang around studios begging for money to bet with. If you raise a hand to help him, why, I'm finished with you."

"I assure you," said Sir John in his most pompous manner, "that this young man has asked for nothing more than a letter of introduction. I have a duty – "

"Stop!" said the woman. "You've a duty to me, too. Hold fast to your money. Likely as not, you'll do neither with 'Take A Chance' Anderson floating around."

It was not her words, neither the contempt in her voice nor the insult which stung him. The man who went twenty rounds with Kid Muldoon had learnt to control his temper, but there was a new factor present – a factor who wore a plain grey dress, and had two big, black eyes which were now solemnly surveying him.

"Lady Maxell," he said, "it is pretty difficult to give the lie to any woman, but I tell you that what you say now is utterly false. I had no intention when I came to Bournemouth of asking for anything that would cost Sir John a penny. As to my past, I suppose it has been a little eccentric, but it is clean, Lady Maxell."

He meant no more than he said. He had no knowledge of Sadie O'Grady's antecedents, or he might not have emphasised the purity of his own. But the woman went back as though she had been whipped, and Timothy had a momentary vision of a charging fury, before she flung herself upon him, tearing at his face, shrieking aloud in her rage…

"Phew!" said Timothy.

He took off his hat and fanned himself. It was the first time he had ever run away from trouble, but now he had almost flown. Those favoured people who were in sight of Sir John Maxell's handsome villa, saw the door swung open and a young man taking the front path in four strides and the gate in another before he sped like the wind along the street.

"Phew!" said Timothy again.

He went the longest way back to his hotel, to find that a telephone message had been received from Sir John. It was short and to the point.

"Please don't come again."

Timothy read the slip and chuckled.

"Is it likely?" he asked the page who brought the message.

Then he remembered the girl in grey, with the dark eyes, and he fingered his smooth chin thoughtfully.

"I wonder if it is worthwhile taking a chance," he said to himself, and decided that, for the moment, it was not.

10

Lady Maxell yawned and put down the magazine she was reading. She looked at her watch. It was ten o'clock. At such an hour Paris would be beginning to wake up. The best people would still be in the midst of their dinner, and Marie de Montdidier (born Hopkins) would be putting the final dabs of powder on her nose in her dressing-room at the Folies Bergères before making her first and her final appearance.

The boulevards would be bright with light, and there would be lines of twinkling autos in the Bois for the late diners at the Aromonville. She looked across at the girl sitting under a big lamp in a window recess, a book on her knees, but her mind and eyes elsewhere.

"Mary," she said, and the girl, with a start, woke from her reverie.

"Do you want me, Lady Maxell?"

"What is the matter with Sir John? You know him better than I do."

The girl shook her head.

"I hardly know, Lady Maxell – "

"For heaven's sake don't call me 'Lady Maxell,' " said the other irritably. "I've told you to call me Sadie if you want to." There was a silence. "Evidently you don't want," snapped the woman. "You're what I call a fine, sociable family. You seem to get your manners from your new friend."

The girl went red.

"My new friend?" she asked, and Lady Maxell turned her back to her with some resolution and resumed for a moment the reading of her magazine.

"I don't mind if you find any pleasure in talking to that kind of insect," she said, putting the periodical down again. "Why, the world's full of those do-nothing boys. I suppose he knows there's money coming to you."

The girl smiled.

"Very little, Lady Maxell," she said.

"A little's a lot to a man like that," said the other. "You mustn't think I am prejudiced because I was – er – annoyed the other day. That is temperament."

Again the girl smiled, but it was a different kind of smile, and Lady Maxell observed it.

"You can marry him as far as I am concerned," she said. "These sneaking meetings are not exactly complimentary to Sir John, that's all."

The girl closed her book, walked across to the shelf and put it away before she spoke.

"I suppose you're speaking of Mr Anderson," she said. "Yes, I have met him, but there has been nothing furtive in the meetings. He stopped me in the park and apologised for having been responsible for the scene – for your temperament, you know."

Lady Maxell looked up sharply, but the girl met her eyes without wavering.

"I hope you aren't trying to be sarcastic," complained the older woman. "One never knows how deep you are. But I can tell you this, that sarcasm is wasted on me."

"I'm sure of that," said the girl.

Lady Maxell looked again, but apparently the girl was innocent of offensive design.

"I say I met Mr Anderson. He was very polite and very nice. Then I met him again – in fact, I have met him several times," she said thoughtfully. "So far from his being a do-nothing, Lady Maxell, I think you are doing him an injustice. He is working at the Parade Drug Store."

"He will make a fine match for you," said the woman. "Sir John will just love having a shop walker in the family!"

That ended the conversation for both of them, and they sat reading for a quarter of an hour before Lady Maxell threw her magazine on the floor and got up.

"Sir John had a telegram yesterday that worried him," she said. "Do you know what it was about?"

"Honestly I do not know, Lady Maxell," said the girl. "Why don't you ask him yourself?"

"Because he would tell me a lie," said the woman coolly, and the girl winced.

"He brought all his money and securities from the Dawlish and County Bank today and put them in his safe and he had the chief constable with him for half an hour this morning."

This was news to the girl, and she was interested in spite of herself.

"Now, Mary," said Lady Maxell, "I'm going to be frank with you – frankness pays sometimes. They called my marriage a romance of the screen. Every newspaper said as much and I suppose that is true. But the most romantic part of the marriage was my estate in Honolulu, my big house in Paris and my bank balance. Ellsberger's publicity man put all that stuff about, and I've an idea that Sir John was highly disappointed when he found he'd married me for myself alone. That's how it strikes me."

Here was a marriage which had shocked Society and had upset the smooth current of the girl's life, placed in an entirely new light.

"Aren't you very rich?" she asked slowly, and Sadie laughed.

"Rich! There was a tram fare between me and the workhouse the day I married Sir John," she said. "I don't blame him for being disappointed. Lots of these cinema stars are worth millions – I wasn't one of them. I married because I thought I was going to have a good time – lots of money and plenty of travel – and I chose with my eyes shut."

The girl was silent. For once Sadie Maxell's complaint had justification. Sir John Maxell was not a spending man. He lived well, but never outside the circle of necessity.

The girl was about to speak, when there came a dramatic interruption.

There was a "whang!" a splintering of glass and something thudded against the wall. Lady Maxell stood up as white as death.

"What was that?" she gasped.

The girl was pale, but she did not lose her nerve.

"Somebody fired a shot. Look!"

She pulled aside the curtain. "The bullet went through the window."

"Keep away from the window, you fool!" screamed the woman. "Turn out the light! Ring the bell!"

Mary moved across the room and turned the switch. They waited in silence, but no other shot was fired. Perhaps it was an accident. Somebody had been firing at a target…

"Go and tell my husband!" said Sadie. "Quickly!"

The girl passed through the lighted hall upstairs and knocked at Sir John's door. There was no answer. She tried the door, but found it locked. This was not unusual. He had a separate entrance to his study, communicating by a balcony and a flight of stairs with the garden. A wild fear seized her. Possibly Sir John had been in the garden when the shot was fired; it may have been intended for him. She knocked again louder, and this time she heard his step and the door was opened.

"Did you knock before?" he asked. "I was writing– "

Then he saw her face.

"What has happened?" he demanded.

The girl told him, and he made his way downstairs slowly, as was his wont. He entered the drawing-room, switched on the lights, and without a glance at his wife walked to the window and examined the shattered pane.

"I imagined I heard a noise, but thought somebody had dropped something. When did this happen? Just before you came up?"

The girl nodded.

Maxell looked from one to the other. His wife was almost speechless with terror, and Mary Maxell alone was calm.

"It has come already," he said musingly. "I did not think that this would happen so soon."

He walked down to the hall where the telephone hung and rang through to the police station, and the girl heard all he said.

"Yes, it is Sir John Maxell speaking. A shot has just been fired through my window. No, not at me – I was in my study. Apparently a rifle shot. Yes, I was right – "

Presently he came back.

"The police will be here in a few moments to make a search of the grounds," he said, "but I doubt whether they will catch the miscreant."

"Is it possible that it was an accident?" asked the girl.

"Accident?" He smiled. "I think not," he said dryly. "That kind of accident is liable to happen again. You had better come up to my study, both of you, till the police arrive," he said and led the way up the stairs.

He did not attempt to support his wife, though her nerve was obviously shaken. Possibly he did not observe this fact until they were in the room, for after a glance at her face he pushed a chair forward.

"Sit down," he said.

The study was the one room to which his wife was seldom admitted. Dominated as he was by her in other matters, he was firm on this point. It was perhaps something of a novelty for her – a novelty which will still the whimper of the crying child has something of the same effect upon a nervous woman.

The door of the safe was open and the big table was piled high with sealed packages. The only money she saw was a thick pad of bank-notes fastened about with a paper bandage, on which something was written. On this she fixed her eyes. She had never seen so much money in her life, and he must have noticed the attention this display of wealth had created, for he took up the money and slipped it into a large envelope.

"This is your money, Mary," he beamed over his glasses at the girl.

She was feeling the reaction of her experience now and was trembling in every limb. Yet she thought she recognised in this diversion an attempt on his part to soothe her, and she smiled and tried hard to respond.

They had been daily companions since she was a mite of four, and between him and his dead brother's child there was a whole lot of understanding and sympathy which other people never knew.

"My money, uncle?" she asked.

He nodded.

"I realised your investments last week," he said. "I happened to know that the Corporation in which the money stood had incurred very heavy losses through some error in insurance. It isn't a great deal, but I couldn't afford to let you take any further risks.

"There was, of course, a possibility of this shot having been fired by accident," he went on, reverting to the matter which would naturally be at the back of his mind. Then he fell into thought, pacing the room in silence.

"I thought you were out," he said, stopping suddenly in front of the girl. "You told me you were going to a concert."

Before she could explain why she changed her mind they heard the sound of voices in the hall.

"Stay here," said Sir John. "It is the police. I will go down and tell them all there is to know."

When her husband had gone, Lady Maxell rose from her chair. The table, with its sealed packages, drew her like a magnet. She fingered them one by one, and came at last to the envelope containing Mary's patrimony. This she lifted in her hands, weighing it. Then, with a deep sigh, she replaced the package on the table.

"There's money there," she said, and Mary smiled.

"Not a great deal, I'm afraid. Father was comparatively poor when he died."

"There's money," said Lady Maxell thoughtfully; "more than I have ever seen since I have been in this house, believe me."

She returned, as though fascinated, and lifted the envelope again and peered inside.

"Poor, was he?" she said. "I think you people don't know what poverty is. Do you know what all this means?"

She held the envelope up and there was a look in her face which the girl had never seen before.

"It means comfort, it means freedom from worry, it means that you don't have to pretend and make love to men whom you loathe."

The girl had risen and was staring at her.

"Lady Maxell!" she said in a shocked voice. "Why – why – I never think of money like that."

"Why should you?" said the woman roughly, as she flung the package on the table. "I've been after money in quantities like that all my life. It has always been dangling in front of me and eluding me – eluding is the word, isn't it?" she asked carelessly.

"What are all those pictures?" she changed the subject abruptly, pointing to the framed photographs which covered the walls. "They're photographs of India, aren't they?"

"Morocco," said the girl. "Sir John was born in Morocco and lived there until he went to school. He speaks Arabic like a native. Did you know that?"

"Morocco," said Lady Maxell. "That's strange. Morocco!"

"Do you know it?" asked the girl.

"I've been there – once," replied the other shortly. "Did Sir John go often?"

"Before he married, yes," said Mary. "He had large interests there at one time, I think."

Sir John came back at that moment, and Mary noticed that his first glance was at the table.

"Well, they've found nothing," he said, "neither footprints nor the empty shell. They're making a search of the grounds tomorrow. Lebbitter wanted to post a man to protect the house in view of the other matter."

"What other matter?" asked his wife quickly.

"It is nothing," he said, "nothing really which concerns you. Of course, I would not allow the police to do that. It would make the house more conspicuous than it is at present."

He looked at the two.

"Now," he said bluntly, "I think you had better go off to bed. I have still a lot of work to do."

His wife obeyed without a word, and the girl was following her, when he called her back.

"Mary," he said, laying his hand upon her shoulder, "I'm afraid I'm not the best man that ever lived, but I've tried to make you happy, my dear, in my own way. You've been as a daughter to me."

She looked up at him with shining eyes. She could not trust herself to speak.

"Things haven't gone as well as they might during the past year," he said. "I made a colossal blunder, but I made it with my eyes open. It hasn't been pleasant for either of us, but there's no sense in regretting what you cannot mend. Mary, they tell me that you've been seeing a lot of this young man Anderson?"

She was annoyed to find herself going red when there was really no reason for it. She need not ask who "they" were, she could guess.

"I've been making inquiries about that boy," said Sir John slowly, "and I can tell you this, he is straight. Perhaps he has led an unconventional life, but all that he told Sadie was true. He's clean, and, Mary, that counts for something in this world."

He seemed at a loss how to proceed.

"Anything might happen," he went on. "Although I'm not an old man, I have enemies…"

"You don't mean – "

"I have many enemies," he said. "Some of them are hateful, and I want to tell you this, that if trouble ever comes and that boy is within call – go to him. I know men, good, bad and indifferent; he's neither bad nor indifferent. And now, good night!"

He kissed her on the forehead.

"You needn't tell your aunt what I've been talking about," he said at parting and led her to the door, closing and locking it behind her.

He sat down in his chair for a very long time before he made a move, then he began picking up the packages and carrying them to the safe. He stopped half-way through and resumed his seat in the chair, waiting for the hour to pass, by which time he judged the household would be asleep.

At midnight he took a pair of rubber boots from a locker, pulled them on, and went out through the door leading to the balcony, down the covered stairway to the garden. Unerringly he walked across the lawn to a corner of his grounds which his gardeners had never attempted to cultivate. He stopped once and groped about in the bushes for a spade which he had carefully planted there a few nights before. His hand touched the rotting wood of an older spade and he smiled. For six years the tool had remained where he had put it the last time he had visited this No-Man's-Land.

Presently he came to a little hillock and began digging. The soil was soft, and he had not gone far before the spade struck wood. He cleared a space two feet square and drew from the earth a small crescent of wood. It was, in fact, a part of the wooden cover of a well which had long since gone dry but which had been covered up by its previous owner and again covered by Maxell.

Lying at full length on the ground, he reached down through the aperture, and his fingers found a big rusty nail on which was suspended a length of piano wire. At the end of the wire was attached a small leather bag and this he drew up and unfastened, and putting the bag on one side, let the free end of the wire fall into the well.

He replaced the wood, covered it again with earth, all the time exercising care, for, small as the aperture was, it was big enough for even a man of his size to slip through.

A cloaked figure which stood in the shadow of the bushes watching him, which had followed him as noiselessly across the lawn, saw him lift the bag and take it back to the house and disappear through the covered stairway. So still a night it was, that the watcher could hear the click of the lower door as Sir John locked it, and the soft pad of his feet as they mounted the stairs.

11

Mr Goldberg, the manager and proprietor of the Parade Drug Store, was a man who possessed neither a sense of imagination nor the spirit of romance. He sent peremptorily for Timothy, and Timothy came with a feeling that all was not well.

"Mr Anderson," said Goldberg in his best magisterial manner, "I took you into my shop because I was short of a man and because I understood that you had had some business experience."

"I have business experience," said Timothy carefully, "of a kind."

"I gave you particular instructions," said Mr Goldberg solemnly, "on one very vital point. We carry a full line of all the best proprietorial medicines, and our customers can always get them upon application. Each of those medicines we duplicate, as you know, providing the same constituents and charging some sixpence to a shilling less – in fact, we are out to save the public from being robbed."

"I understand you," said Timothy, "but I don't see much difference between robbing the public and robbing the patent medicine proprietors, and all that just-as-good stuff never did impress me, anyway. It stands to reason," he said, leaning over the desk and speaking with the earnestness of a crusader, "that the advertised article must be more even in quality and it must be good all round. You can't advertise a bad article and get away with it, except on the first sale, and that doesn't pay the advertiser. The goods sell the goods, and the advertisement is only to make you take the first lick."

"I do not want a lecture on advertising or on commercial morality," said Mr Goldberg with ominous calm. "I merely want to tell you that you were overheard by my chief assistant telling a customer not to 'take a chance' on one of my own pills."

"That's right," said Timothy, nodding his head vigorously. "Guilty, my lord. What about it?"

"I have had a further complaint," said Mr Goldberg, consulting with elaborate ceremony a little note-book. "I understand that you have initiated the awful practice of offering to toss customers for their change. People have written me strong letters of complaint about it."

"Because they lost," said the indignant Timothy; "what's wrong about that, anyway, Mr Goldberg? I don't pocket the money, and I win twice out of every three times. If a fellow likes to take a chance as to whether he gets sixpence or we get a shilling, why worry?"

The outraged Mr Goldberg brindled.

"That sort of thing may be all right at a country fair or even in a country shop," he said, "but it is not good enough for the Parade Drug Store, Bournemouth, and I'll dispense with your services as from this morning."

"You're losing a good man," said Timothy solemnly, but Mr Goldberg did not seem to take that loss to heart.

All "Take A Chance Anderson's" jobs ended violently. He never conceived of them ending in any other way, and invariably regarded the sum of money which was received in lieu of notice, or as compensation for breach of contract, as being something in the nature of a nest-egg which a kindly Providence had foreordained, and he was neither cast down nor elated by the crisis in his affairs when, by a fortunate accident, he met Mary Maxell – the fortune was apparent, but the accident belonged to the category which determined the hour at which trains leave stations.

Hitherto, on the girl's part, these meetings had been fraught with a certain amount of apprehension, if not terror. They had begun when Timothy had stopped her on the morning after his quarrel with Lady Maxell, and had made bland inquiries as to that lady's condition. Then she had been in a panic and frantically anxious to end the interview, and it required all her self-restraint to prevent her flying at top speed from this wicked young man who had been so abominably rude.

At their second meeting he had greeted her as an old friend, and she had left him with the illusion of a life-time acquaintance. Hereafter matters went smoothly, and they went so because Timothy Anderson was unlike any of the other boys she had ever met.

He paid her no compliments, he did not grow sentimental, he neither tried to hold her hand nor kiss her, nor was he ever oppressed by that overwhelming melancholy which is the heritage and pride of youth.

Not once did he hint at an early decline or the possibility of his going away to die in far lands. Instead he kept her in screams of laughter at his interpretation of movie plays in the making. He did not ask for a keepsake; the only request he made of her in this direction was one which first took her breath away. Thereafter she never met him unless she had in the bag which slung from her wrist one small box of matches; for "Take A Chance" Anderson had never possessed or carried the means of ignition for his cigarette for one whole hour together.

Timothy told her most of what the proprietor of the Parade Drug Store had told him. The girl thought it was a joke, because that was exactly the way Timothy presented the matter.

"But you won't be going away soon?" she asked.

"Not till I go abroad," replied Timothy calmly.

"Are you going abroad too?" she asked in surprise.

He nodded.

"I'm going to Paris and Monte Carlo – especially to Monte Carlo," he said, "and afterwards I may run across to Algeria or to Egypt."

She looked at him with a new respect. She was less impressed by the great possessions which his plans betrayed than by his confident independence, and dimly she wondered why he was working at a drug store for low wages and wondered, too, whether he was –

"What are you blushing about?" asked Timothy curiously.

"I wasn't blushing," she protested; "I was just wondering whether I could ever afford a trip like that."

"Of course you can," said the young man scornfully. "If I can afford it, you can, can't you? If I go abroad and stay at the best hotels, and go joy rides in the Alps and plan all this when I haven't got fifteen shillings over my rent – "

"You haven't fifteen shillings over your rent!" she repeated, aghast. "But how can you go abroad without money?"

Timothy was genuinely astounded that she could ask so absurd a question.

"Why, I'd take a chance on that," he said. "A little thing like money doesn't really count."

"I think you're very silly," she said. "Oh, there was something I wanted to tell you, Mr Anderson."

"You may call me Timothy," he said.

"I don't want to call you Timothy," she replied.

He shook his head with a pained expression.

"It'll be ever so much more sociable if you call me Timothy and I call you Mary."

"We can be very sociable without that familiarity," she said severely. "I was just going to tell you something."

They sat on the grass together, on the shadow fringe of a big oak and the spring sunshine wove its restless arabesques on her lap.

"Do you know," she said after a pause, "that last night I had two queer experiences and I was scared; oh, scared to death!"

"Eating things at night," said Timothy oracularly, "especially before you go to bed – "

"I wasn't dreaming," she said indignantly, "nor was it a nightmare. I won't tell you if you're so horrid."

"I'm only speaking as an ex-chemist and druggist," said Timothy gravely; "but please forgive me. Tell me what it is, Mary."

"Miss Maxell," she said.

"Miss Mary Maxell," he compromised.

"First I'll tell you the least worst," she began. "It happened about one o'clock in the morning. I had gone to bed awfully tired, but somehow I couldn't sleep, so I got up and walked about the room. I didn't like putting on the light because that meant drawing down the blinds which I had let up when I went to bed, and the blinds make such a noise that I thought the whole of the house would hear. So I put on my dressing-gown and sat by the window. It was rather chilly, but my wrap was warm, and sitting there I dozed. I don't know how long, but it was nearly an hour, I think. When I woke up I saw a man right in the centre of the lawn."

Timothy was interested.

"What sort of a man?"

"That is the peculiar thing about it," she said. "He wasn't a white man."

"A coon?" he asked.

She shook her head.

"No, I think it must have been a Moor. He wore a long white dress that reached down to his ankles, and over that he had a big, heavy black cloak."

Timothy nodded.

"Well?"

"He went round the corner of the house towards uncle's private stairway and he was gone quite a long time. My first thought was to awaken uncle and tell him, but then I remembered that Sir John had spent a long time in Morocco and possibly he knew that the man was about the house. You see, we have had Moorish visitors before, when ships have come to Poole. Once we had a very important man, a Kaid, and Sir John made queer tea for him in glasses with mint and stuff. So I just didn't know what to do. Whilst I was wondering whether I ought not at least to wake Lady Maxell, he reappeared, walked across the lawn and went down the path which leads to the back entrance – you're laughing at me," she said suddenly.

"What you mistake for a laugh," said Timothy solemnly, "is merely one large smile of pleasure at being in your confidence."

She was in two minds as to whether she would be angry or pleased, but his tone changed to a more serious one.

"I don't like the idea of the gaudy East wandering loose under your bedroom window in the middle of the night," he said. "Did you tell Lady Maxell this morning?"

The girl shook her head.

"No, she was up very early and has been out all day. I have not seen her – in fact, she was not at breakfast. Now I'll tell you the really serious thing that happened, and I do hope, Mr Anderson, that you won't be flippant."

"Trust me," said Timothy.

The girl had no reason to complain of his attitude when she had described the shooting incident. He was aghast.

"That is terrible!" he said vigorously. "Why, it might have hit you!"

"Of course it might have hit me," she said indignantly. "That's the whole point of my story, so far as you are concerned – I mean, so far as I am concerned," she added hastily.

"So far as I am concerned too," said Timothy quietly. "I just hate the idea of anything even frightening you."

She rose hurriedly.

"I am going to shop now," she said.

"What's the hurry?" grumbled Timothy.

"Mr Anderson," she said, ignoring his question, "I don't want you to think that uncle is feeling badly about you because of what has happened in the house. He spoke to me of you last night, and he spoke very nicely. I am worried to death about Sir John. He has made enemies in his life, and I am sure that this shooting affair is the sequel to some old feud."

Timothy nodded.

"I should say that is so," he said.

He looked down at the grass very thoughtfully and then:

"Well, I'll go home," he said. "I had better sleep this afternoon if I am to be up all night."

"Up all night?" she said in surprise. "What is happening? Is there a ball or something?"

"There will be something livelier than a ball," he said grimly, "if I find anybody in your garden tonight. And Miss Maxell, if you look out of your window and you see a solitary figure on sentry-go don't shoot, because it will be me."

"But you mustn't," she gasped. "Please don't do it, Mr Anderson. Uncle would be – "

He stopped her with a gesture.

"Possibly nobody will come tonight," he said, "and as likely as not I shall be pinched by the police as a suspicious character. But there's a chance that somebody will come, and that's the chance I'm going to take."

12

True to his word, he returned to his lodgings and spent the afternoon in slumber. He had the gift which all great men possess, of being able to sleep at will. He was staying at a boarding-house, and occupied a room which had originally been a side veranda, but had been walled in and converted into an extra bedroom. It was a remarkably convenient room for him, as he had discovered on previous occasions. He had but to open the window and drop on to the grass to make his exit without anybody in the house being the wiser. More to the point, he could return at any hour by the same route without disturbing the household.

He had his supper, and whilst it was still very light he went out to reconnoitre Sir John's demesne. He was able to make the circuit of the house, which occupied a corner site and was isolated by two lanes, and he saw nobody until, returning to the front of the house, a car drove up and a woman alighted.

He had no difficulty in recognising Lady Maxell, but the taxi interested him more than the lady. It was smothered with mud and had evidently come a long journey.

As evidently she had hired it in some distant town and she had not as yet finished with it, because she gave the man some directions and money, and from the profound respect which the chauffeur showed, it was clear that that money was merely a tip.

Timothy stood where he could clearly be seen, but her back was toward him all the time and she did not so much as glance in his direction when she passed through the gate and up the garden path.

It was curious, thought Timothy, that she did not take the car up the drive to the house. More curious was it that she should, at this late hour of the evening, have further use for it.

He returned to his room, full of theories, the majority of which were wholly wild and improbable. He lay on his bed, indulging in those dreams which made up the happiest part of his life. Of late he had taken a new and a more radiant pattern to the web of his fancy and –

"Oh, fiddlesticks!" he said in disgust, rolling over and sitting up with a yawn.

He heard the feet of the boarders on the gravel path outside, and once he heard a girl say evidently to a visitor: "Do you see that funny room! That is Mr Anderson's."

There was still an hour or so to be passed, and he joined the party in the parlour so restless and distrait as to attract attention and a little mild raillery from his fellow guests. He went back to his room, turned on the light and pulled a trunk from under the bed.

Somehow his mind had been running all day upon that erring cousin whose name he bore and whose disappearance from public life was such a mystery. Possibly it was Sir John's words which had brought Alfred Cartwright to his mind. His mother had left him a number of family documents, which, with the indolence of youth, he had never examined very closely. He had the impression that they consisted in the main of receipts, old diplomas of his father's (who was an engineer) and sundry other family documents which were not calculated to excite the curiosity of the adventurous youth.

He took out the two big envelopes in which these papers were kept and turned them on to the bed, examining them one by one. Why his cousin should be in his mind, why he should have taken this action at that particular moment, the psychologist and the psychical expert alone can explain. They may produce in explanation such esoteric phenomena as auras, influences, and telepathies, and perhaps they are right.

He had not searched long before he came upon a small package of newspaper cuttings, bound about by a rubber band. He read them at first without interest, and then without comprehension. There was one cutting, however, which had been clipped from its context, which seemed to tell the whole story of the rest. It ran:

> When Cartwright stood up for sentence he did not seem to be greatly troubled by his serious position. As the words 'twenty years' passed Mr Justice Maxell's lips, he fell back as if he had been shot. Then, springing to the edge of the dock, he hurled an epithet at his lordship. Some of his business associates suggest that the learned judge was a partner of Cartwright's – an astonishing and most improper suggestion to make. In view of the statement that the prisoner made before the trial, when suggestions had been made in a newspaper that the judge had been connected with him in business years before, and remembering that Cartwright's statement was to the effect that he had had no business transactions with the judge, it seems as though the outburst was made in a fit of spleen at the severity of the sentence. Sir John Maxell, after the case, took the unusual step of informing a Press representative that he intended placing his affairs in the hands of a committee for investigation, and had invited the Attorney-General to appoint that committee. 'I insist upon this being done,' he said, 'because after the prisoner's accusation I should not feel comfortable until an impartial committee had examined my affairs.' It is understood that after the investigation the learned judge intends retiring from the Bench.

Timothy gasped. So that was the explanation. That was why Maxell had written to him, that was why he made no reference at all to his father, but to this disreputable cousin of his. Slowly he returned the package to its envelope, dropped it into his trunk and pushed the trunk under the bed.

And that was the secret of Cousin Cartwright's disappearance. He might have guessed it; he might even have known had he troubled to look at these papers.

He sat on the bed, his hands clasping his knees. It was not a pleasant reflection that he had a relative, and a relative moreover after whom he was named, serving what might be a life sentence in a convict establishment. But what made him think of the matter tonight?

"Mr Anderson! Timothy!"

Timothy looked round with a start. The man whose face was framed in the open window might have been forty, fifty or sixty. It was a face heavily seamed and sparsely bearded – a hollow-eyed, hungry face, but those eyes burnt like fire. Timothy jumped up.

"Hullo!" he said. "Who are you 'Timothying'?"

"You don't know me, eh?" the man laughed unpleasantly. "Can I come in?"

"Yes, you can come in," said Timothy.

He wondered what old acquaintance this was who had come to the tramp level, and rapidly turned over in his mind all the possible candidates for trampdom he had met.

"You don't know me, eh?" said the man again. "Well, I've tracked you here, and I've been sitting in those bushes for two hours. I heard one of the boarders say that it was your window and I waited till it was dark before I came out."

"All this is highly interesting," said Timothy, surveying the shrunken figure without enthusiasm, "but who are you?"

"I had a provisional pardon," said the man, "and they put me in a sanatorium – I've something the matter with one of my lungs. It was always a trouble to me. I was supposed to stay in the sanatorium – that was one of the terms on which I was pardoned – but I escaped."

Timothy stared at him with open mouth.

"Alfred Cartwright!" he breathed.

The man nodded.

"That's me," he said.

Timothy looked down at the edge of the black box.

"So that is why I was thinking about you," he said. "Well, this beats all! Sit down, won't you?"

He pulled a chair up for his visitor and again gazed on him with curiosity but without affection. Something in Timothy's attitude annoyed Cartwright.

"You're not glad to see me?" he said.

"Not very," admitted Timothy. "The truth is, you've only just come into existence so far as I am concerned. I thought you were dead."

"You didn't know?"

Timothy shook his head.

"Not until a few minutes ago. I was reading the cuttings about your trial – "

"So that was what you were reading?" said the man. "I'd like to see 'em one of these days. Do you know what I've come for?"

It was only at that moment that Sir John flashed through Timothy's mind.

"I guess what you've come after," he said slowly. "You're here to see Sir John Maxell."

"I'm here to see Mister Justice Maxell," said the man between his teeth. "You're a good guesser."

He took the stump of a cigar from his waistcoat pocket and lit it.

"John Maxell and I have a score to settle, and it is going to be settled very soon."

"Tide and weather permitting," said Timothy flippantly, recovering his self-possession. "All that vendetta stuff doesn't go, Mr Cartwright." Then he asked in a flash: "Did you shoot at him last night?"

The man's surprise was a convincing reply.

"Shoot at him? I only got to this place this afternoon. It's more likely he's waiting to shoot at me, for the sanatorium people will have telegraphed to him the moment I was missing."

Timothy walked to the window and pulled down the blinds.

"Now tell me, Mr Cartwright, before we go any farther, do you still persist in the story you told the court, that the judge was a party to your swindle?"

"A party to it!" said the other man furiously. "Of course he was! I was using the money of my companies to buy concessions from the Moorish Government, as much on his behalf as on mine. He wasn't in the Brigot swindle – but he held shares in the company I was financing. We located a gold mine in the Angera country, and Maxell and I went across to Europe every year regularly to look after our property.

"We had to keep it quiet because we secured the concessions from the Pretender, knowing that he'd put the Sultan out of business the moment he got busy. If it had been known, the Sultan would have repudiated the concession, and our Government would have upheld the repudiation. Maxell speaks the language like a native, and I learnt enough to get on with El Mograb, who is the biggest thing amongst the rebel tribes. El Mograb wanted us to stay there, Maxell and I; he'd have made us shereefs or pashas, and I'd have done it, because I knew there was going to be an investigation sooner or later into the affairs of my companies. But Maxell wouldn't have it. He always pretended that, so far as he knew, my financing was straight. You know the rest," he said. "When I came before Maxell, I thought I was safe."

"But Sir John allowed his affairs to be inspected," said Timothy. "If he had been engaged with you in this Morocco business, there must have been papers to prove it."

Cartwright laughed harshly.

"Of course he'd allow his affairs to be investigated," he sneered. "Do you think that old fox couldn't *cache* all the documents that put him wrong? Papers? Why, he must have enough papers to hang him, if you could only find 'em!"

"What are you going to do?" asked Timothy.

There was one thing he was determined that this man should not do, and that was to disturb the peace of mind, not of Sir John Maxell or his wife, but of a certain goddess whose bedroom overlooked the lawn.

"What am I going to do?" replied Cartwright. "Why, I'm going up to get my share. And he'll be lucky if that's all he loses. One of the mines was sold to a syndicate last year – I had news of it in gaol. He didn't get much for it because he was in a hurry to sell – I suppose his other investments must have been going wrong twelve months ago – but I want my share of that!"

Timothy nodded.

"Then you had best see Sir John in the morning. I will arrange an interview."

"In the morning!" said the other contemptuously. "Suppose you make the arrangement, what would happen? When I went up there I should find a couple of cops waiting to pinch me. I know John! I'm going to see him tonight."

"I think not," said Timothy, and the man stared at him.

"You think not?" he said. "What has it to do with you?"

"Quite a lot," said Timothy. "I merely state that you will not see him tonight."

Cartwright stroked his bristly chin undecidedly and then:

"Oh, well," he said in a milder tone, "maybe you can fix things up for me in the morning."

"Where are you sleeping tonight?" asked Timothy. "Have you any money?"

He had money, a little; and he had arranged to sleep at the house of a man he had known in better times. Timothy accompanied him through the window and into the street, and walked with him to the end of the road.

"If my gamble had come off, you'd have benefited, Anderson," said the man unexpectedly, breaking in upon another topic which they were discussing.

They parted, and Timothy watched him out of sight, then turned on and walked in the opposite direction, to take up his self-imposed vigil.

13

There was something in the air that was electrical, and Mary Maxell felt it as she sat at supper with Sir John and his wife. Maxell was unusually silent and his wife amazingly so. She was nervous and almost jumped when a remark was addressed to her. The old truculence which distinguished her every word and action, her readiness to take offence, to see a slight in the most innocent remark, and her combativeness generally, had disappeared; she was almost meek when she replied to her husband's questions.

"I just went round shopping and then decided to call on a girl I had known a long time ago. She lives in the country, and I felt so nervous and depressed this morning that I thought a ride in a taxi would do me good."

"Why didn't you take our car?" asked the other.

"I didn't decide until the last moment to go out to her, and then I went by train one way."

Sir John nodded.

"I'm glad you went into the fresh air," he said, "it will do you good. The country is not so beautiful as Honolulu, but it is not without its attractions."

It was unusual for the Judge to be sarcastic, but it was less usual for Lady Maxell to accept sarcasm without a retort. To Mary's surprise she made no reply, though a faint smile curved those straight lips of hers for a second.

"Do you think it was a burglar last night?" she asked suddenly.

"Good heavens, no!" said Maxell. "Burglars do not shoot up the house they burgle."

"Do you think it is safe to have all this money in the house?" she asked.

"Perfectly safe," he said. "I do not think that need alarm you."

No further reference was made to the matter, and presently Sir John went up to his study. Mrs Maxell did not go to the parlour, but drew a chair to the fire in the dining-room and read, and the girl followed her example. Presently the elder woman left the room and was gone a quarter of an hour before she returned.

"Mary," she said, so sweetly that the girl was startled, "such an annoying thing has happened – I have lost the key of my wardrobe. You borrowed one of Sir John's duplicates the other day – where did you put the ring?"

John Maxell was a methodical and systematic man. He had a duplicate set of all the keys in the house, and these as a rule were kept in a small wall-safe in his own bedroom. He had never invited his wife to use that receptacle, but she had a shrewd idea that the combination which was denied to her had been given to the girl.

Mary hesitated.

"Don't you think if you asked Uncle – "

"My dear," smiled the lady, "if I went to him now, he'd never forgive me. If you know where the keys are, be an angel and get them for me."

The girl rose, and Lady Maxell followed her upstairs. Her own room was next to her husband's and communicated, but the door was invariably locked on Maxell's side. Presently the girl came in to her.

"Here they are," she said. "Please let me put them back quickly. I feel very guilty at having taken them at all without his permission."

"And for goodness' sake don't tell him," said Lady Maxell, examining the keys.

At last she found the one she wanted, but was a long time in the process. She opened her bureau and the girl took the big key-ring from her hand with such evident relief that Lady Maxell laughed.

It had been easier than she thought and unless she made a blunder, the key she had selected from the bunch while she was fumbling at the bureau, would make just the difference – just the difference.

It was not customary for Sir John to come down from his study to enjoy the ladies' company after dinner, but on this evening he made an exception to his rule. He found his wife and ward reading, one on each side of the fireplace. Lady Maxell looked up when her husband came in.

"Here is a curious story, John," she said. "I think it must be an American story, about a woman who robbed her husband and the police refused to arrest her."

"There's nothing curious about that," said the lawyer, "in law a wife cannot rob her husband or a husband his wife."

"So that if you came to my Honolulu estate and stole my pearls," she said banteringly, "I could not have you arrested."

"Except for walking in my sleep!" he said smilingly, and they both laughed together.

He had never seen her so amiable, and for the first time that day – it had been a very trying and momentous day – he had his misgivings. She, with the memory of her good day's work, the excellent terms she had arranged with the skipper of the *Lord Lawrence*, due to leave Southampton for Cadiz at daylight the next morning, had no misgivings at all, especially when she thought of a key she had placed under her pillow. She had had the choice of two boats, the *Lord Lawrence* and the *Saffi*, but the *Saffi*'s voyage would have been a long one, and its port of destination might hold discomfort which she had no wish to experience.

The household retired at eleven o'clock, and it was past midnight before Sadie Maxell heard her husband's door close, and half an hour later before the click of the switch told her that his light had been extinguished

He was a ready sleeper, but she gave him yet another half-hour before she opened the door of her bedroom and stepped out into the black corridor. She moved noiselessly towards the study, her only fear being that the baronet had locked the door before he came out. But this fear was not well founded, and the door yielded readily to her touch. She was dressed, and carried only a small attaché case filled with the bare necessities for the voyage.

She pushed the catch of her electric lamp, located the safe and opened it with no difficulty. She found herself surprisingly short of breath, and her heart beat at such a furious rate that she thought it must be audible to everybody in the house. The envelope with the money lay at the bottom of the others, and she transferred its contents to her attaché case in a few seconds.

Then her heart stood still…

It was only the faintest creak she heard, but it came from a corner of the room where the door leading to the cupboard stairway was placed. She saw a faint grey line of light appear – the stairway had a glass roof and admitted enough light to show her that the door was slowly opening. She had to bite her lips to stop herself from screaming. To make her escape or to rouse Sir John was impossible, and she opened the attaché case again, and with trembling fingers felt for the little revolver which she had taken from her drawer. She felt safer now, yet she had not the courage to switch on the light.

She saw the figure of a man silhouetted in the opening, then the door closed, and her terror bred of itself a certain courage.

She flashed the light full on his face. The dead silence was broken when she whispered:

"Oh, God! Benson!"

"Who's that?" he whispered, and snatched the torch from her hand.

He looked at her long and curiously, and then:

"I expected to find that Maxell had taken most of my possessions," he said, "but I never thought he would take my wife!"

"Let us see what all this is about," boomed the big voice of John Maxell almost in the man's ear, he was so close, and suddenly the room was flooded with light.

14

The self-appointed watcher found time pass very slowly. Twelve and one o'clock struck from a distant church, and there was no sign of midnight assassins, and the house, looking very solemn and quiet in the light of a waning moon, irritated and annoyed him. From the roadway where he paced silently to and fro – he had taken the precaution of wearing a pair of rubber-soled shoes – he could glimpse Mary's window, and once he thought he saw her looking out.

He made a point of walking entirely round the house twice in every hour, and it was on one of these excursions that he heard a sound which brought him to a standstill. It was a sound like two pieces of flat board being smacked together sharply.

"Tap...tap!"

He stopped and listened, but heard nothing further. Then he retraced his footsteps to the front of the house and waited, but there was no sound or sign. Another half-hour passed, and then a patrolling policeman came along on the other side of the roadway. At the sight of the young man he crossed the road, and Jim recognised an acquaintance of his drug-store days. Nothing was to be gained by being evasive or mysterious, and Timothy told the policeman frankly his object.

"I heard about the shooting last night," said the man, "and the inspector offered to put one of our men on duty here, but Sir John wouldn't hear of it."

He took a professional look at the house, and pointed to its dark upper windows.

"That house is asleep – you needn't worry about that," he said; "besides, it will be daylight in two hours, and a burglar wants that time to get home."

Timothy paused irresolutely. It seemed absurd to wait any longer, and besides, to be consistent he must be prepared to adopt this watchman role every night.

There was no particular reason why Sir John Maxell's enemy should choose this night or any other. He had half expected to see Cartwright and was agreeably disappointed that he did not loom into view.

"I think you're right," he said to the policeman. "I'll walk along down the road with you."

They must have walked a quarter of a mile, and were standing chatting at the corner of the street, when a sound, borne clearly on the night air, made both men look back in the direction whence they had come. They saw two glaring spots of light somewhere in the vicinity of the Judge's house.

"There's a car," said the officer, "what is it doing there at this time of the morning? There is nobody sick in the house, is there?"

Timothy shook his head. Already he had begun to walk back, and the policeman, sensing something wrong, kept him company. They had covered half the distance which separated them from the car, when it began to move toward them, gathering speed. It flashed past and Timothy saw nothing save the driver, for the hood was raised and its canvas blinds hid whatever passenger it carried.

"It came in from the other end of the avenue," said the policeman unnecessarily. "Maybe Sir John is going a long journey and is starting early."

"Miss Maxell would have told me," said Timothy, troubled. "I nearly took a chance and made a jump for that car."

It was one of the few chances Timothy did not take, and one that he bitterly regretted afterwards.

"If you had," said the practical policeman, "I should have been looking for the ambulance for you now."

Timothy was no longer satisfied to play the role of the silent watcher. When he came to the house he went boldly through the gate and up the drive, and his warrant for the intrusion was the officer who followed him. It was then that he saw the open window of the girl's room, and his heart leapt into his mouth. He quickened his step, but just as he came under the window, she appeared, and Timothy sighed his relief.

"Is that you?" she said in a low worried voice; "is that Mr Anderson? Thank heaven you've come! Wait, I will come down and open the door for you."

He walked to the entrance, and presently the door was opened and the girl, dressed in a wrapper, appeared. She tried to keep her voice steady, but the strain of the past half-hour had been too much for her, and she was on the verge of tears when Timothy put his arm about her shaking shoulders and forced her down into a chair.

"Sit down," he said, "and tell us what has happened."

She looked at the officer and tried to speak.

"There's a servant," said the policeman; "perhaps he knows something."

A man dressed in shirt and trousers was coming down the stairs.

"I can't make him hear," he said, "or Lady Maxell, either."

"What has happened?" asked Timothy.

"I don't know, sir. The young lady woke me and asked me to rouse Sir John."

"Wait, wait," said the girl. "I am sorry I am so silly. I am probably making a lot of trouble over nothing. It happened nearly an hour ago, I was asleep and I heard a sound; thought I was dreaming of what happened last night. It sounded like two shots, but, whatever it was, it woke me."

Timothy nodded.

"I know. I thought I heard them too," he said.

"Then you were out there all the time?" she asked and put out her hand to him.

For that look she gave him Timothy would have stayed out the three hundred and sixty-five nights in the year.

"I lay for a very long time, thinking that the sound would wake my uncle, but I heard nothing."

"Is your room near Sir John's?" asked the policeman.

"No, mine is on this side of the building; Sir John and Lady Maxell sleep on the other side. I don't know what it was, but something alarmed me and filled me with terror – something that made my flesh go rough and cold – oh, it was horrible!" she shuddered.

"I couldn't endure it any longer, so I got out of bed and went out into the corridor to wake uncle. Just then I heard a sound outside my window, but I was just too terrified to look out. Then I heard a motor-car and footsteps on the path outside. I went to Sir John's door and knocked, but got no answer. Then I tried Lady Maxell's door, but there was no answer there either. So I went to Johnson's room and woke him," she looked at Timothy, "I – I – thought that you might be there, so I came back to the open window and looked."

"Show me Sir John's room," said the policeman to the servant, and the three men passed up the stairs, followed by the girl.

The door which the man indicated was locked, and even when the policeman hammered on the panel there was no response.

"I think the key of my door will unlock almost any of the room doors," said the girl suddenly. "Sir John told me once that all the room locks were made on the same plan."

She went away and came back with a key. The policeman fitted it in the lock and opened the door, feeling for and finding the electric switch as he entered. The room was empty, and apparently the bed had not been occupied.

"Where does that door lead?" he asked.

"That leads to Lady Maxell's room," said the girl; "there is a key on this side."

This door he found was open and again they found an empty room and a bed which had not been slept in. They looked at one another.

"Wouldn't Sir John be in his study till late?" asked Timothy.

The girl nodded.

"It is at the end of the corridor," she said in a broken voice, for she felt that the study held some dreadful secret.

This door was locked too, locked from the inside. By now the policeman was standing on no ceremony, and with a quick thrust of his shoulder he broke the lock, and the door flew open.

"Let us have a little light," he said, unconsciously copying words which had been spoken in that room an hour before.

The room was empty, but here at any rate was evidence. The safe stood open, the fireplace was filled with glowing ashes, and the air of the room was pungent with the scent of burnt paper.

"What is this?" asked Timothy, pointing to the ground.

The floor of the study was covered with a thick, biscuit-coloured carpet, and "this" was a round, dark stain which was still wet. The policeman went on his knees and examined it.

"It is blood," he said briefly; "there's another patch near the door. Where does this door lead? Catch that girl, she's fainting!"

Timothy was just in time to slip his arm round Mary's waist before she collapsed. By this time the household was aroused, and a woman servant was on the spot to take charge of Mary. When Timothy had rejoined the policeman, that officer had discovered where the door led.

"You go down a stairway into the garden," he said. "It looks as if two shots were fired here. Look, there's the mark of both of them on the wall."

"Do you suggest that two people have been killed?"

The policeman nodded.

"One was shot in the middle of the room, and one was probably shot on the way to the door. What do you make of this?" and he held up a bag, discoloured and weather-worn, with a handle to which was fastened a long length of rusty wire.

"It is empty," said the officer, examining the contents of the little grip which, up till an hour before, had held John Maxell's most jealously guarded secrets.

"I'll use this phone," said the officer. "You'd better stay by, Mr Anderson. We shall want your evidence – it will be important. It isn't often we have a man watching outside a house where a murder is committed – probably two."

The sun had risen before the preliminary interrogation and the search of the house and grounds had been concluded. Blewitt the detective, who had taken charge of the case, came into the dining-room, where a worried servant was serving coffee for the investigators, and dropped down on to a chair.

"There's one clue and there's one clue alone," he said, and drew from his pocket a soft hat. "Do you recognise this, Anderson?"

Timothy nodded.

"Yes," he said, "that was worn last night by the man I spoke to you about."

"Cartwright?" said the detective.

"I could swear to it," said Timothy. "Where did you find it?"

"Outside," said the detective; "and that is all we have to go on. There is no sign of any body. My first theory stands."

"You believe that the murderer carried Sir John and Lady Maxell into the car and drove away with them?" said Timothy; "but that presupposes that the chauffeur was in the plot."

"He may have been and he may have been terrorised," said the detective. "Even a taxi driver will be obliging if you stick a gun in his stomach."

"But wouldn't Miss Maxell have heard – " began Timothy.

"Miss Maxell heard," said the detective, "but was afraid to look out. She also heard two shots. My theory is that Sir John and Lady Maxell were killed, that the murderer first locked both the bedrooms, went through Sir John's papers, presumably to discover something incriminating himself, and to destroy such documents."

"But why not leave the bodies?" said Timothy.

"Because without the bodies no indictment of murder could hold against him."

Timothy Anderson turned as the girl came in. She was looking very tired, but she was calmer than she had been earlier in the morning.

"Is there any news?" she asked, and Timothy shook his head.

"We have searched every inch of the ground," he said.

"Do you think – " She hesitated to ask the question.

"I am afraid," replied Timothy gently, "that there is very little hope."

"But have you searched everywhere?" insisted the girl.

"Everywhere," replied Timothy.

Soon after, Timothy took the girl away to an hotel for breakfast and to arrange for a room, and the house was left in charge of the police. Later came the famous detective Gilborne, who made an independent search, but he, like his predecessors, failed to discover any further evidence, because he also knew nothing of the disused well, which lay hidden under a rubbish heap.

15

Who killed Sir John Maxell and his wife? Where had their bodies been hidden? These were the two questions which were to agitate England for the traditional space of nine days. For one day, at any rate, they formed the sole topic of speculation amongst the intelligent section of fifty million people.

The first question was easier to answer than the second. It was obvious to the newsmen that the murderer was Cartwright, whose threats of vengeance were recalled and whose appearance at Bournemouth had been described at second hand by the detective in charge of the case. First-hand information was for the moment denied the pressmen, for Timothy, fully dressed, lay on his bed in a sound sleep. Happily for him, neither then nor later did any of the enterprising newspaper men associate the "A C" in his name with the wanted criminal. He was at least spared that embarrassment.

But the story of his vigil as "a friend of Sir John's" was in print long before he woke up to find a small and impatient army of reporters waiting to interview him. He answered the reporters' interrogations as briefly as possible, bathed and changed and made his way to the hotel where the girl was. She was leaving as he arrived, and the warmth of her greeting almost banished the depression which lay upon him. She put her arm through his so naturally that he did not realise his wonderful fortune.

"I've got something to tell you," she said, "unless you know already. All my money has gone."

He stopped with a gasp.

"You don't mean that?" he said seriously.

"It is true," she replied. "I believe it was very little and my loss is so insignificant compared with the other awful affair that I am not worrying about it."

"But Sir John had money?"

She shook her head.

"I have just seen his lawyers," she said, "they have been to the bank and there is not a hundred pounds to his credit, and that amount will be absorbed by the cheques he has drawn. He drew a very, very large sum, including my money, from the bank two days ago. You know," she went on, "I think that Sir John contemplated leaving for America? He had already given me a hint, asking me how long it would take me to pack my belongings, and I fancy that had something to do with the telegram he received – "

"Announcing Cartwright's escape," nodded Timothy.

"He was so kind and so gentle," said the girl, her eyes filling with tears, "that to me he was more like a father. Oh, it is awful, awful!"

"But you?" asked the agitated Timothy. "What are you going to do? Good heavens! It is dreadful!"

"I shall have to work," said the girl practically and with a little smile. "I do not think that will kill me. Hundreds of thousands of girls have to work for their living, Timothy, and I shall have to work for mine."

Timothy drew a long breath.

"Not if I can help it, you won't," he said. "I am sure I shall make a lot of money. I can feel it in my bones. If a man takes a job – "

"You mustn't talk like that," she said, pressing his arm, "and anyway, how could I let you help me or keep me? That sort of thing isn't done – not by nice girls."

She laughed, but became sober again.

"Do you know that Sir John was very much interested in you?"

"In me?" said Timothy.

She nodded.

"I told you so the other day. I think he liked you, because he was saying how uncomfortable you must be at Vermont House, living in that queer little room of yours."

Timothy was startled.

"How did he know I was living at Vermont House?" he said.

She smiled.

"Vermont House happens to be Sir John's property," she said. "In fact, I think it is the only realisable piece of property he has, now that the money has gone."

"What shall you do immediately?" asked Timothy.

She shook her head.

"I don't know," she replied. "I think the first step is to get out of this hotel, which is much too expensive for me. I have a few pounds in the bank, but that won't last very long."

At his earnest entreaty she agreed to see a solicitor and appoint him to save whatever was possible from the wreckage of Sir John's estate. Two hours passed like as many minutes, until Timothy remembered that he had an appointment with a London reporter – one Brennan. Brennan he had known in his cinema days, and Timothy literally fell upon his neck.

"I've nothing to tell the boys that hasn't already been told," he said, putting down the newspaper which Brennan handed to him. "I am as anxious for news as you are. Have there been any developments?"

"None," said the reporter, "except that Sir John had no money at the bank and no money could be found in the house."

Timothy nodded.

"That I know," he said, "all his securities were drawn out two days ago. That was the stuff that Cartwright was after."

"Does Miss Maxell know – " Brennan began.

"She does know and she took it like a brick."

"It was about twenty thousand pounds," Brennan went on. "The only other clue the police have is that the safe was opened by Maxell's duplicate key. The old man had two sets made, one of which he used to keep in his combination safe in his bedroom and the other he carried around with him. Miss Maxell told a story that the night before the murder Lady Maxell asked her to secure possession of the keys in order to open a bureau."

Timothy nodded.

"I see. Is it suggested that Lady Maxell detached the key of the safe and that it was she who opened it?"

"That is one theory," said the other, "the police have miles of 'em! They've got everything except the bodies and the murderer. Now come out with that story, Anderson! You must know a great deal more than you've told, and I'm simply without a new fact that these evening papers haven't got, to hang my story on. Why did Cartwright come to your room, anyway? Do you know him?"

"He was an acquaintance of my father's," said Timothy diplomatically, "and perhaps he thought I knew Maxell better than I did."

"That sounds pretty thin," said the reporter. "Why should he come to you?"

"Suppose I am the only person he knew or knew about," said Timothy patiently. "Suppose he'd been all round Bournemouth trying to find a familiar name."

"There's something in that," admitted the reporter.

"Anyway," said Timothy, "I was a kid when he went to gaol. You don't imagine I knew him at all, do you?"

He had gone out to meet the girl, forgetting to take his watch, and now he was looking round for it.

"Here is a theory," said Brennan suddenly. "Suppose Lady Maxell isn't dead at all."

"What do you mean?" asked the other.

"Suppose Cartwright killed Maxell and Lady Maxell witnessed the murder. Suppose this fellow had to decide whether he would kill the witness or whether he would go away with her? You said the motor-car which came to the house in the middle of the night was the same as that in which Lady Maxell came home. Isn't it likely that she should have told the murderer, for some reason or other, that the car was coming, because evidently she had arranged for it to come, and that they went away together? Isn't it likely, too, that she was in the plot, and that, so far from being a victim, she was one of the criminals? We know her antecedents. There was some trouble over her stabbing a young American, Reggie van Rhyn. In fact, most of the evidence seems to incriminate her. There is the key, for example. Who else but she could have taken the duplicate key? Doesn't it look as though she planned the whole thing, and that her accomplice came in at the last moment to help her get away and possibly to settle Sir John?

"Take the incident of the two locked bedrooms. Obviously somebody who lived in the house and who knew the family routine must have done that. Both Sir John and Lady Maxell were in the habit of fastening their doors at night, and the servants did not go into the bedrooms unless they were rung for. It seems to me fairly clear that Lady Maxell locked the doors so that the suspicions of the servants should not be aroused in the morning."

"If I had your powers of deduction," said the admiring Timothy, "I should never miss a winner. Where the blazes is my watch?"

"Try under the pillow," said Brennan.

"I never put it there," replied Timothy, but nevertheless turned the pillow over and stood gaping.

For beneath the pillow was a long, stout envelope with a tell-tale blood stain in one corner.

"For heaven's sake!" breathed Timothy, and took up the package.

It bore no address and was sealed.

"What on earth is this?" he asked.

"I can tell you what those stains are," said the practical Brennan. "Is there any name on it?"

Timothy shook his head.

"Open it," suggested the reporter, and the other obeyed.

The contents were even more astonishing, for they consisted of a thick pad of money. They were new Bank of England notes and were bound about by a tight band of paper. On the band was written in Sir John's handwriting:

Proceeds of the sale of stocks held in trust for Miss Mary Maxell. £21,300.

The detective in charge of the case was a man of many theories. But his new theory was an uncomfortable one for Timothy Anderson.

"This puts a new light upon the case," said the detective, "and I'm being perfectly frank with you, Mr Anderson, that the new light isn't very favourable to you. Here you are, outside the building when the crime is committed. You are seen by a policeman a few minutes after the shots are fired, and a portion of the money stolen from the house is discovered under your pillow."

"Discovered by me," said Timothy, "in the presence of a witness. And are you suggesting that, whilst I was with your policeman, I was also driving the car, or that I was wearing Cartwright's cap which was found in the grounds? Anyway, you've the finger-print of your man and you're at liberty to compare it with mine."

"It isn't a finger-print anyway," said the detective, "it is the print of a knuckle and we do not keep a record of knuckles. No, I admit that the motor-car conflicts a little bit with my theory. Have you any suggestion to offer?"

Timothy shook his head.

"The only suggestion I can make," he said, "is that Cartwright, in a hurry to get away and knowing the position of my room, hid the money there for fear he should be caught with the goods. At any rate, if I were the criminal I would not hide a blood-stained envelope under my pillow. I should at least have the intelligence to burn the envelope and put the money where the servants of this house could not find it. Why, don't you see," he said vigorously, "that any of the servants at this boarding-house would have found the envelope if I hadn't?"

The detective scratched his head.

"There's something in that," he said. "It is a very queer case."

"And it is being investigated by very queer people," said Timothy irritably.

A little further investigation, however, relieved Timothy of all suspicion. He had not returned to the house until ten o'clock that morning. The maid, who had taken him a cup of tea at eight, noticing that he had been out all night, thought it was an excellent opportunity to straighten the room to "get it off her mind," as she said. She did not remake the bed, but had tidied it. Whilst sweeping she had seen the envelope lying on the floor near the open window and had picked it up and, for want of a better place, thinking "it was private" had slipped it under Timothy's pillow.

As Timothy had not been out of sight of the police since the tragedy until his return to his lodgings, there could be no suggestion that he had any part in hiding the envelope. Whatever irritation he felt was dispelled by his large and generous satisfaction when the poverty which threatened Mary was averted. But why should Cartwright hide the money there? Why should he stop in his headlong flight to come to the window, as evidently he did, and throw the package into the room? There were a hundred places where he might have left it.

"That cousin stuff doesn't work," thought Timothy, "and if you think he's going to rely upon his relationship with me and can use me to look after his money, he's made one large mistake."

He saw the girl again at the official inquiry, and met her on the day after. She was going to Bath where she had some distant relations, and they had met to say goodbye.

It was a gloomy occasion – less gloomy for Timothy than for the girl, because he was already planning a move to the town in which she was taking up her quarters. This cheerful view was banished, however, when she explained that her stay in Bath was merely a temporary expedient.

"Mrs Renfrew has wired asking me to come – and it seems as good a place as any for a few months. I don't think I shall stay here any longer," she said. "I want a change of air and a change of scene. Timothy, I feel that I shall never get over Sir John's death."

"Never is a very long time, my dear," said Timothy gently, and she could only wonder at the tender kindness in his voice.

She had little time to wonder, however, for she had a proposition to make to him and she hardly knew how to reduce it to words.

"Are you – are you – working?" she asked.

Timothy's broad smile answered her plainly that he was not.

"The fact is," he said airily, "I haven't quite decided what I am going to do. If you were going down to Bath for good, I was going down to Bath also. Maybe I could start a druggist's or buy a store, or run errands for somebody. I am the most accommodating worker."

"Well – " she began and stopped.

"Well?" he repeated.

"I had an idea that maybe you would like to go on and conduct an independent search – independent of the police, I mean – and find something about the man who killed Sir John, and perhaps bring him to justice. You know, I think you are clever enough," she went on hurriedly, "and it would be work after your own heart."

He was looking at her steadily.

"Quite right, Mary," he said quietly, "but that involves spending a whole lot of money. What misguided person do you suggest would send me out on that kind of job?"

"Well, I thought – " She hesitated, and then a little incoherently, "You see, I have the money – mainly through you – my own money, I mean. I feel I have a duty to my poor uncle and I could trust you to do your very best. I could afford it, Timothy" – she laid her hand on his arm and looked up at him almost beseechingly – "indeed I can afford it. I have more money than I shall ever spend."

He patted her hand softly.

"Mary," he said, "it is just the kind of job I should like, and with anybody's money but yours, why, I'd be out of the country in two shakes, looking for Mr Cartwright in the most expensive cities of the world. But, my dear, I cannot accept your commission, because I know just what lies behind it. You think I'm a restless rather shiftless sort of fellow, and you want to give me a good time – with your money."

He stopped and shook his head.

"No, my dear," he said, "thank you, but, no!"

She was disappointed and for a moment a little hurt.

"Would two hundred pounds – " she suggested timidly.

"Not your two hundred," he said. "That lawyer of yours should take better care of your money, Mary. He shouldn't allow you to make these tempting offers to young men," he was smiling now. "Will you go abroad?"

"Perhaps – some day," she said vaguely. "Sir John wanted me to go – and I feel that I should be pleasing him. Some day, yes, Timothy."

He nodded.

"Maybe I'll go over at the same time as you," he said. "I thought of taking a chance in Paris for a while – you can make big money in Paris."

"In – a while?" she smiled.

"In a minute," said Timothy grimly, "if the horse and the jockey are of the same way of thinking. I know a fellow who races pretty extensively in France. He has a horse called Flirt – "

She held out her hand for the second time.

"Timothy, you're incorrigible," she said.

She did not see him again for twelve months, not indeed until, after a winter spent in Madeira, she put her foot over the gangway of the SS *Tigilanes* and met the quizzical smile of the youth who was waiting to receive her.

For Timothy had been in Funchal a month, seeing but unseen, since Mary was generally in bed before the Casino woke up and play reached any exciting level.

16

Timothy sat now on an upturned trunk, his elbows on the rails of the SS *Tigilanes* and his speculative eye roving the river front of Liverpool.

It was the last hour of the voyage, and Timothy, who had left Funchal with four hundred pounds in his pocket-book, had exactly three genuine shillings and a five-milreis piece of dubious quality.

A man strolled along the deck and fell in at his side.

"Cleaned you out last night, didn't they?" he asked sympathetically.

"Eh? Oh, yes, I believe they did. That red-haired man had all the luck and most of the cards."

He smiled and Timothy had a swift, happy smile that brought tired little ridges under his eyes. He was not only good-looking and young, but he was interesting.

The man at his side took the cigar from his teeth and looked at it before he spoke.

"Of course, you know they were crooks – they work this coast line regularly."

"Eh?"

Timothy looked round, shocked and pained.

"You don't say? Crooks! What, that little red-haired fellow who has been trying to pick a quarrel with me all the voyage, and the tall, nice-looking Englishman?"

His companion nodded.

"Don't you remember the Captain warned us not to play cards – "

"They always do that to be on the safe side," said Timothy, but he was obviously uneasy. "Of course, if I knew they were crooks – "

"Knew! Good lord! Anybody will tell you. Ask the purser. Anyway, you've been stung and you can do nothing. The best thing to do is to grin and bear your losses. It is experience."

Timothy felt the three honest shillings in his pocket and whistled dismally.

"Of course, if I were sure – "

He turned abruptly away and raced down the main companionway to the purser's little office under the stairs.

"Mr Macleod, I want to see you."

"Yes, sir," – all pursers are a little suspicious, – "anything wrong with your bill?"

"No – not unless his name's Bill. Shall I come in?"

The purser opened the half-door and admitted him to the sanctuary.

"There are two fellows aboard this packet – a red-haired fellow named Chelwyn and a disguised duke named Brown – what do you know about 'em?"

The purser made a face. It was intended to convey his lack of real interest in either.

"I'll put it plainly," said the patient Timothy. "Are they crooks?"

"They play cards," said the purser diplomatically.

He desired at this the eleventh hour to avoid scandal, explanations, and such other phenomena which he associated in his mind with the confrontation of the wise men and their dupes. That sort of thing brought the Line into disrepute, and indirectly reflected upon the ship's officers. Besides, the ship was making port, and, like all pursers, he was up to his eyes in work and frantically anxious to clear it off in a minimum time so that he could take a train to his little villa at Lytham, where his family was established.

"I'm sorry, Mr Anderson, if you've been stung," he said, "but the captain gives fair warning the first night out of Cape Town and Madeira – that's where you came aboard, isn't it? – and there were notices posted up, both in the saloon and in the smoking-room. Have you lost much?"

He looked up with some sympathy at the tall, athletic figure with the tired, smiling eyes.

"I cleared up £500 at the Funchal Casino," said Timothy, "and I reckon I have spent £100 legitimately."

"The rest is gone, eh?" said the purser. "Well, Mr Anderson, I am afraid I can do nothing. The best thing to do is to mark it down against 'Experience'."

"I'll forgive you for being philosophical about my losses," said Timothy. "Will you be kind enough to tell me the number of Mr Chelwyn's cabin?"

"Two seventy-four," said the purser. "I say, Mr Anderson, if I were you I'd let the matter drop."

"I know you would, dear old thing," said Timothy, shaking him warmly by the hand, "and if I were you I should let it drop too. But, as I am me – 274, I think you said?"

"I hope you're not going to make any trouble, Mr Anderson," said the alarmed purser. "We've done our best to make you comfortable on the voyage."

"And I did my best to pay for my ticket, so we're quits," and with a wave of his hand Timothy strode out of the cabin, dodged down past the steward carrying up the luggage to the next deck, and walked swiftly along the carpeted corridor till he found a little number-plate bearing the figures "274." He knocked at the cabin door, and a gruff voice said, "Come in!"

Chelwyn, the red-haired man, was in his shirt sleeves, fastening his collar. Brown was sitting on the edge of his bunk, smoking a cigarette, and Chelwyn, who had seen Timothy reflected in the mirror as he came in, was first to recognise him.

"Hullo, Mr Anderson, do you want anything?" he asked politely. "Sorry you've had such bad luck – what the devil are you doing?"

Timothy had shut the door and slipped the bolt.

"Yes, I want something," he said. "I want four hundred pounds."

"You want – "

"Listen. I thought you were playing straight, you fellows, or I wouldn't have played with you. I'm willing to take a chance, for that's my motto in life, dear lads, but there isn't a chance to take when you're playing with crooks."

"Look here," said the red-haired man, walking over to him and emphasising his words with his forefinger against Timothy's chest, "that kind of stuff doesn't amuse me. If you lose your money, lose it like a sportsman and a gentleman, and don't squeal."

Timothy grinned.

"Boys," he said, "I want four hundred pounds from you, so step lively."

The suave Mr Brown, who had been watching the scene with bored eyes, stroking his drooping moustache the while, made a gentle entrance into the conversation.

"I'm rather surprised, in fact, I am shocked, Mr Anderson, that you should take this line," he said. "You've lost your money fairly and squarely – "

"That's where you're lying," said Timothy pleasantly. "Now, I'm telling you this. We're very near the shore. Somewhere at the back of those warehouses there's certain to be a police organisation and a well-paid magistrate. You are going to have a grand opportunity of appearing in the respectable part of the court as a prosecutor, for I'm going to beat you up – first you," he pointed to the red-haired Chelwyn, "and then you."

"You're going to beat me up, are you?" said the red-haired man and made a quick dive.

It was not pretty to watch, unless you took an interest in fighting. They closed for a second and something jolted twice under Chelwyn's jaw. He fell back against the cabin partition. He leapt again, but Timothy's fist met him half-way, and he never really felt what hit him.

"I've won this fight," said Timothy, "and I award myself a purse of four hundred pounds. Do you take any interest in these proceedings, Brown?"

The other man had not moved from his bunk, but now he rose and lifted his dazed companion to his feet.

"We'd better pay this fellow."

"I'll see him – " mumbled the other, but Brown was apparently the brains of the organisation and had merely mentioned his intention of paying out of sheer politeness to his companion.

He took a thick pocket-book from his hip pocket and counted out the notes, and Timothy picked them up.

"I'll fix you for this," said Chelwyn, mopping his bleeding lip. "You've taken this from me – not him."

"Don't frighten me," said Timothy as he unbolted the door and stepped out.

"Some day I'll get you," said the livid man, and the finger he pointed at Timothy was shaking with anger.

"I'll take a chance on that," said Timothy.

He ascended the companion-way feeling remarkably cheerful, and met the purser coming down. That officer regarded him even more suspiciously than ever. But as there were no signs of the fray upon him, the purser went to his cabin relieved, and Timothy passed out to relieve his feelings by the side of the rail. So he sat whilst the big liner was brought alongside the wharf, and then he heard his name spoken and jumped up, hat in hand.

"I just wanted to tell you, Timothy, in case I did not see you on the train," she remarked, "that Mrs Renfrew has decided not to go back to Bath but to go on to Paris almost immediately."

"Good for Mrs Renfrew," said Timothy. "Bath or Paris will find me hanging around. I nearly came down to you just now to borrow my fare to Bath."

"Timothy," she said in a shocked voice, "did you lose all the money you won in Funchal?"

Timothy rubbed his nose.

"I didn't exactly lose it," he said. "I lent it and it has just been repaid."

"Mrs Renfrew doesn't think it proper your travelling on the same boat. She thinks you ought not to have come to Madeira after me – us."

There was mischief in Mary's eyes, in spite of the solemnity of her tone.

"I shouldn't worry about what Mrs Renfrew thinks," said Timothy. "Why, you're almost as badly off for cousins as I am."

"As you are?" she said in surprise. "Have you any cousins?"

"Hundreds of 'em," said Timothy glibly.

"Who are they?" she asked, interested.

She had reached a stage in their friendship when his relatives were immensely interesting.

"I don't know their names," lied Timothy. "I don't give 'em names but numbers – one, two, three, four, etc. – just at that moment I was thinking of number seventy-nine – good morning, Mrs Renfrew."

Mrs Renfrew was severe and thin, with a yellow face and hooked nose. She was a member of one of the best, if not the best, families in Bath, and it was an unfailing source of pride that she did not know the people that other people knew.

Mary watched the encounter with dancing eyes.

"Shall I have the pleasure of your company to London?" asked Mrs Renfrew.

She invariably made a point of leaving Mary out, and indeed sustained the pleasant fiction that Mary had no existence on board the ship.

"The pleasure will be mine," said Timothy. "I am not travelling with you to London."

He said this so innocently that Mrs Renfrew was in the middle of her next observation before she had any idea that the remark had an offensive interpretation.

"You seem to have had a very unfortunate experience – what do you mean?"

Happily a very hot-looking steward made his appearance at that moment and called Mrs Renfrew away. She gathered up her charge and with a withering glance at Timothy departed.

"Take A Chance" Anderson, feeling particularly happy, was one of the first to land and strolled along the quay-side waiting within view of the gangway for Mary to disembark. Immediately above him towered the high decks of the *Tigilanes* – a fact of which he was reminded when, with a crash, a heavy wooden bucket dropped so close to his head that it grazed his shoulder. It was a large bucket, and, dropped from that height, might have caused him considerable physical distress.

He looked up.

The two card-players with whom he had had some argument were lolling over the rail, their faces turned in quite another direction and talking earnestly.

"Hi!" said Timothy.

They were deaf, it appeared, for they still continued their discussion. A deck hand was passing with a crate load of oranges; one fell out and Timothy picked it up. The attention of Messrs Chelwyn and Brown was still directed elsewhere, and with a little swing of his arm Timothy sent the orange upon its swift and unerring course. It caught the red-haired man square in the side of the face and burst, and he jumped round with an oath.

"You've dropped your bucket," said Timothy sweetly. "Shall I throw it at you or will you come down and get it?"

The man said something violent, but his companion pulled him away, and Timothy went to look for a seat with peace in his heart.

17

The train was crowded, but he secured a corner seat in one of the cell-like compartments. It was empty when he entered, but immediately after, to his surprise, Brown and Chelwyn followed him in and deposited their goods upon three seats that they might in the manner of all experienced travellers, occupy breathing space for three at the cost of two tickets.

They took no notice of Timothy until the train drew out and he wondered what their game was. It was hardly likely that they would start any rough work with him after their experience of the morning and less likely because these boat trains were well policed.

Clear of the Riverside Station the smooth Englishman leant forward.

"I hope, Mr Anderson," he said, "that you will forget and forgive."

"Surely," said Timothy, "I have nothing to forgive."

"My friend," said Mr Brown with a smile, "is very precipitate – which means hasty," he explained.

"Thank you," said Timothy, "I thought it meant crooked."

A spasm contorted the features of Mr Chelwyn, but he said nothing. As for Brown, he laughed. He laughed heartily but spuriously.

"That's not a bad joke," he said, "but to tell you the truth, we mistook you for – one of us, and my friend and I thought it would be a good joke to get the better of you."

"And was it?" asked Timothy.

"It was and it wasn't," said Mr Brown, not easily nonplussed. "Of course, we intended restoring the money to you before you left the ship."

"Naturally," said Timothy. "I never thought you would do anything else."

"Only you know you rather spoilt our little *esprit*."

"If the conversation is to develop in a foreign language," said Timothy, "I would only remark: *Honi soit qui mal y pense*," and the polite Mr Brown laughed again.

"You do not mind if my friend and I have a little quiet game by ourselves, if," he said humorously, "we swindle one another."

"Not at all," said Timothy. "I have no objection to watching, but if," he said cheerfully, "you should suddenly draw my attention whilst your friend's head is turned, to the ease with which I could win a hundred pounds by picking the lady, or discovering the little pea under the little shell, or show me a way of getting rich from any of the other devices which the children of the public schools find so alluring at the country fair, I shall be under the painful necessity of slapping you violently on the wrist."

Thereafter the conversation languished until the train had run through Crewe and was approaching Rugby. It was here that Mr Brown stopped in the midst of a long, learned discussion on English politics to offer his cigarette-case to Timothy. Timothy chose a cigarette and put it in his pocket.

"That is one of the best Egyptian brands made," said Mr Brown casually.

"Best for you or best for me?" asked Timothy.

"Bah!" It was the red-haired Chelwyn who addressed him for the first time. "What have you to be afraid of? You're as scared as a cat! Do you think we want to poison you?"

Mr Brown produced a flask and poured a modicum of whisky into the cup and handed it to his companion, then he drank himself. Then, without invitation be poured a little more into the cup and offered it to Timothy.

"Let bygones be bygones," he said.

"I have no desire to be a bygone," said Timothy, "I would much rather be a herenow."

Nevertheless, he took the cup and smelt it.

"Butyl chloride," he said, "has a distinctive odour. I suppose you don't call it by its technical name, and to you it is just vulgarly 'a knock-out drop.' Really," he said, handing back the cup, "you boys are so elementary. Where did you learn it all – from the movies?"

The red-haired man half rose from his seat with a growl.

"Sit down," said Timothy sharply, and with a jerk of his hand he flung open the carriage door.

The men shrank back at the sight of the rapidly running line, and at the certainty of death which awaited any who left the train on that side of the carriage.

"Start something," said Timothy, "and I'll undertake to put either one or both of you on to the line. We're going at about sixty miles an hour, and a fellow that went out there wouldn't be taking a chance. Now is there going to be a rough house?"

"Close the door, close the door," said Mr Brown nervously. "What a stupid idea, Mr Anderson!"

Timothy swung the door to and the man moved up towards him.

"Now, I'm just going to put it to you plainly," said Brown. "We've made the voyage out to the Cape and the voyage back and the only mug we met was you. What we won from you just about paid our expenses, and I'm putting it to you, as a sportsman and a gentleman, that you should let us have half of that stuff back."

"The sportsman in me admires your nerve," said Timothy, "but I suppose it is the gentleman part that returns an indignant 'No!' to your interesting observation."

Brown turned to his companion.

"Well, that's that, Len," he said, "you'll just have to let the money go. It is a pity," he said wistfully and his companion grunted.

That ended the conversation so far as the journey was concerned, and Timothy heard no more until he was in the gloomy courtyard at Euston Station and stepping into his taxi.

To his surprise it was the red-haired man who approached him, and something in his manner prevented Timothy from taking the action which he otherwise would have thought necessary.

"Look here, young fellow," he said, "you watch Brown – he's wild."

"You're not exactly tame," smiled Timothy.

"Don't take any notice of me," said the man a little bitterly. "I am engaged in the rough work. I should have got two hundred out of your money – that's what made me so wild. Brown paid all my expenses and gives me ten pound a week and a commission. It sounds funny to you, doesn't it, but it is the truth," and somehow Timothy knew that the man was not lying.

"He's finished with me – says I am a hoodoo," said the little man. "Do you know what I've got out of five weeks' work? Look!"

He held out his hand and disclosed two ten-pound notes.

"Brown's dangerous," he warned Timothy. "Don't you make any mistake about that. I was only wild because I was losing my money, but he's wild because you've got fresh with him and caught him out every time. Good night!"

"Here, wait," said Timothy.

He felt in his pocket.

"If you're lying, it is a plausible lie and one that pleases me," he said. "This will salve my conscience."

He slipped two notes into the man's hands.

Chelwyn was speechless for a moment. Then he asked:

"And where are you staying in London, Mr Anderson?"

"At the Brussell Hotel."

"At the Brussell Hotel," repeated the other, "I'll remember that. I shall hear if anything is going on and I'll phone you. You're a gentleman, Mr Anderson."

"So Mr Brown said," remarked Timothy and drove off, feeling unusually cheerful.

If Timothy could be cheerful under the depressing conditions which prevailed on the night of his arrival in London, he was a veritable pattern of cheer. A drizzling rain was falling as the taxi squeaked its way through a labyrinth of mean streets. He had glimpses of wretched-looking people, grotesque of shape and unreal, through the rain-blurred window of the cab.

Then suddenly the character of the streets changed, and he was in a broad street twinkling with light. There was a glimpse of trees, wide open spaces, dotted with light. The street grew busier and the traffic thicker, then suddenly the cab turned again into semi-darkness and pulled up before the hotel.

A porter opened the door.

"What do I think of Madeira?" asked Timothy of the astonished man. "I haven't had time to think. Will I be staying long in London? No. What are my opinions of the political crisis which has arisen in my absence? I would rather not say."

It takes a great deal to upset the equilibrium of a well-conducted hall man.

"Have you booked your room?" he asked.

Timothy meekly admitted that he had.

He woke to a London much more beautiful, to a vista of old-world buildings such as Cruikshank loved to draw, to a green square and glimpses of greener trees.

Mary was staying at the Carlton, but he had arranged to meet her for lunch. He had not arranged to meet her dragon, but he knew she would be there. He had breakfasted, and was on the point of leaving the hotel, when Chelwyn came.

To say that Timothy regretted his generosity of the night before would be to do him an injustice. Nevertheless, he had some misgivings as to whether he had not been a little too generous. The appearance of Mr Chelwyn, early in the morning, looking so spruce and confident, was in itself a suspicious happening, though events proved that the suspicion was unfounded.

"Can I see you alone for a moment, Mr Anderson?" asked the red-haired man.

Timothy hesitated.

"Come along to the drawing-room," he said.

It was the one public room which would be empty at that time of the morning. Mr Chelwyn deposited his hat and stick and brand-new yellow gloves before he spoke.

"Now, Mr Anderson, I've come to tell you a few facts which will surprise you."

"You haven't had a gold brick sent to you by your Uncle George in Alaska, have you?" asked Timothy dubiously. "Because I'm not buying that kind of fact."

The man smiled and shook his head.

"It is hardly likely I should try that stuff on you, sir," he said. "No, this is a much more serious matter. Before I go any farther I'll tell you that I am not asking for money. I am grateful to you for what you did to me last night, Mr Anderson. A crook has a wife and children the same as anybody else. I have been in this funny business for ten years, but now I'm out of it for good." He looked round and dropped his voice. "Mr Anderson, I told you last night that we've been five or six weeks away from England. Didn't that sound strange to you?"

"Not to me," said Timothy.

"That is because you don't know the game," said the man. "As a rule, when we're working these liners, we go out to Cape Town and come back by the next ship that sails. What do you think we stayed at Funchal for – there's no money in short voyages – it's all on the long run from Madeira to Cape Town."

"I haven't the slightest idea," said Timothy wearily. "I don't even remember seeing you in Funchal – "

"We laid low," interrupted the man.

"That may be, but if you've come to tell me the interesting story of your life, Ginger, I beg that you will cut it short – the history, I mean, not necessarily your life."

"Well, I'll tell it to you as quickly as possible," said the man. "I don't always work with Brown. In fact, I've only worked with him about three times before. I'm not as good a man with the broads – "

"The broads?" said the puzzled Timothy.

"With the cards," corrected the man. "I say that I'm not as good a man with the broads as some of the others. I've got a bit of a reputation for scrapping. I've never left a pal in the lurch and I've always been ready for any 'rough house' that came along. About two months ago Brown sent for me – he's got a flat off Piccadilly and lives like a lord. He told me he was going to Madeira on a special job, that he'd been employed by a lady in Paris – a Madame Serpilot (you'd better write that down in your pocket-book) – to shepherd a young lady who was coming over. Mind you, there was no harm intended to the young lady, but the general idea was that she might be accompanied by a man, and he was the fellow who had to be looked after."

"What was the lady's name?" asked Timothy quickly.

"Miss Maxell," said the man without hesitation, "and you were the fellow we were asked to put out of business. Brown's idea was to break you; then, when you got to London, one of his pals would have met you and offered to lend you money. They'd have framed up a charge against you of obtaining money by false pretences, and you would have been pinched."

Timothy's eyebrows rose.

"Was this Mrs Serpilot's plan?" he asked, but the man shook his head.

"No, sir, she just gave the details to Brown. She never said what was to be done to you, according to him, but you were to be stopped going around with the young lady."

"Who is Madame Serpilot?"

"There you've got me," said Chelwyn. "I believe she's an old widow, but Brown never told me much about her. He got instructions from her while he was in Paris, but I never discovered how. I went to Madeira with him because he knew I was tough – but I wasn't tough enough," he added with a dry smile.

Timothy held out his hand.

"Ginger," he said solemnly, "please forgive the orange!"

"Oh, I didn't mind that," said the man, "that's all in the day's work. It made me a bit wild, and my eye's feeling sore, but don't let that worry you. What you've got to do now is to look out for Brown, because he'll have you as sure as death."

"I'll look out for Madame Serpilot, too," said Timothy. "I think I'll go to Paris."

"She's not in Paris now, I can tell you that," said the man. "The wire Brown got at Liverpool was from Monte Carlo."

"Monte Carlo," said Timothy, "is even more attractive than Paris."

18

Chelwyn left Timothy with something to think about. Who was Madame Serpilot, this old lady who had such an interest in Mary travelling alone? And why, oh! why had she left Paris for Monte Carlo at the fag end of the season? For he and Mary had privately decided between them that London and Paris should only be stopping places on the route to the Riviera. Why should Madame Serpilot have changed her plans at the same time? There was something more than a coincidence in this. At lunch-time he had Mary to herself, her chaperon having a headache.

"Mary," he said, "can you tell me why we changed our plans on the boat and decided to go straight on to Monte Carlo instead of staying in Paris?"

"Yes," she said readily. "Don't you remember my telling you about those beautiful books of views that I saw on the ship?"

"Where did you see them?" asked Timothy.

"I found them in my cabin one day. I think the steward must have left them," she said. "They were most wonderful productions, full of coloured prints and photographs – didn't I tell you about them?"

"I remember," said Timothy slowly. "Found them in your cabin, eh? Well, nobody left any beautiful or attractive pictures of Monte Carlo in my berth, but I think that won't stop me going on to Monte Carlo."

It was an opportunity she had been seeking for a week and she seized it.

"I want to ask you something, Timothy," she said. "Mrs Renfrew told me the other day that they call you 'Take A Chance' Anderson. Why is that, Timothy?"

"Because I take a chance, I suppose," he smiled. "I've been taking chances all my life."

"You're not a gambler, Timothy, are you?" she asked gravely. "I know you bet and play cards, but men do that for amusement, and somehow it is all right. But when men start out to make a living, and actually make a living, by games of chance, they somehow belong to another life and another people."

He was silent.

"You're just too good to go that way, Timothy," she went on. "There are lots of chances that a man can take in this world, in matching his brains, his strength and his skill against other men, and when he wins his stake is safe. He doesn't lose it the next day or the next month, and he's picking winners all the time, Timothy."

His first inclination was to be nettled. She was wounding the tender skin of his vanity, and he was startled to discover how tender a skin that was. All that she said was true and less than true. She could not guess how far his mind and inclination were from commonplace labour and how very little work came into the calculations of his future. He looked upon a job as a thing not to be held and developed into something better, but as a stopgap between two successful chances. He was almost shocked when this truth came home to him. The girl was nervous, and painfully anxious not to hurt him, and yet well aware that she was rubbing a sore place.

"Timothy, for your sake, as well as for mine, for you're a friend of mine, I want to be proud of you, to see you past this present phase of life. Mrs Renfrew speaks of you as a gambler, and says your name, even at your age, is well known as one who would rather bet than buy. That isn't true, Timothy, is it?"

She put her hand on his and looked into his face. He did not meet her eyes.

"I think that is true, Mary," he said steadily. "How it comes to be true, I don't quite know. I suppose I have drifted a little over the line, and I'm grateful to you for pulling me up. Oh, no, I don't regret the past – it has all been useful – and I have made good on chances, but I see there are other chances that a man can take than putting his money on the pace of a horse or backing against zero. Maybe, when I get back to London I'll settle down into a respectable citizen and keep hens or something."

He was speaking seriously, though at first she thought he was being sarcastic.

"And you won't gamble again?" she asked.

He hesitated to reply.

"That isn't fair," she said quickly. "I mean it isn't fair of me to ask you. It is almost cruel," she smiled, "to let you go to Monte Carlo and ask you not to put money on the tables. But promise me, Timothy, that when I tell you to stop playing, you will stop."

"Here's my hand on it," said Timothy, brightening up already at the prospect of being allowed to gamble at all. "Hereafter – " He raised his hand solemnly. "By the way," he asked, "do you know a lady named Madame Serpilot?"

She shook her head.

"No, I do not," she said. "I have never heard the name."

"You have no relations or friends in France?"

"None," she replied immediately.

"What made you go to France at all?" he asked. "When I heard from you, Mary, you talked about taking a holiday in Madeira before setting up house in Bath, and the first thing I knew of your intention to go abroad again was the letter you sent me just before I started for Madeira."

"I wanted to go a year ago, after Sir John's death," she said; "then Mrs Renfrew couldn't take the trip – one of her younger children had measles."

"Has that woman children?" asked Timothy in an awed voice.

"Don't be absurd. Of course she has children. It was she who decided on making the trip. She writes little articles in the *Bath County Herald* – a local paper – on the care of children and all that sort of thing. She's not really a journalist, she is literary."

"I know," said Timothy, "sometimes they write poetry, sometimes recipes for ice cream – 'take three cups of flour, a pint of cream in which an egg has been boiled and a pinch of vanilla' – "

The girl smiled. Evidently Timothy had hit upon the particular brand of journalism to which Mrs Renfrew was addicted.

"Well," said the girl, "there was to have been a sort of Mothers' Welfare Meeting in Paris next week – an International affair – and when we were in Madeira she received an invitation to attend with a free return ticket – wasn't that splendid?"

"Splendid," said Timothy absently. "Naturally you thought it was an excellent opportunity to go also."

The girl nodded.

"And now you have arrived here you find that the Mothers' Welfare Meeting has been postponed for ten years?"

She looked at him, startled.

"How did you know that the meeting had been postponed?" she asked.

"Oh, I guessed it," he said airily, "such things have happened before."

"The truth is," said the girl, "nobody knows anything about this meeting, and the letter which Mrs Renfrew sent to the Mothers' Welfare Society in Paris was waiting for us when we arrived at the Carlton. It had been returned – 'Addressee Unknown.' Mrs Renfrew had put the Carlton address inside."

Here was ample excuse for speculation of an innocuous kind. Mrs Renfrew had been approached because it was known by this mysterious somebody that she would take the girl with her, and this sinister somebody had hired two thugs to shepherd her from Madeira and to put Timothy out of action, should he decide to accompany the party to France. The situation was distinctly interesting.

Three days later the party crossed the Channel. Timothy had high hopes of adventure, which were fated to be more than fulfilled. They stayed three days in Paris and he had the time of his life. He went to the races at Maisons Lafitte, and came back glowing with a sense of his virtue, for he had not made a bet. He drifted in to the baccara rooms at Enghien, watched tens of thousands of francs change hands, and returned to Paris that night with a halo fitted by Mary's own hands.

"I think you're really wonderful, Timothy," she said. "You know you are allowed one final flutter."

"I'm saving that up for Monte Carlo," said Timothy.

Since his arrival in Paris he had lost the right to his name, for he was taking no chances. If he went abroad at night he kept to the brilliantly illuminated boulevards or the crowded cafés. He kept clear of the crowds – especially crowds which formed quickly and for no apparent reason.

He was taking no chances because he felt it was not fair upon the particular genius who presided over his destinies that he should squander his luck in a miraculous escape from death or disablement. Only once, when dining at the Scribe, did he think he saw the familiar face of Mr Brown. With an apology he left the two ladies and made his way with difficulty through the crowded restaurant, only to find that his man had disappeared.

"These cafés have as many doors as a trick-scene," he grumbled when he came back.

"Did you see a friend of yours?" asked the girl.

"Not so much a friend as one who has a financial interest in me," replied Timothy.

Mrs Renfrew had thawed a little under the beneficent influences of Paris. She was busy sending off picture-postcards and had written to Bath her first impression of the French capital to the extent of three columns. She had also written a poem which began: "Oh, city of light that shines so bright," and went on rhyming "vain" with "Seine," "gay" with "play," "joy" with "alloy," through twenty-three stanzas.

"I rather pride myself," said Mrs Renfrew, "upon that description of Paris – 'the city of light.' Don't you think it is very original, Mr Anderson?"

"It was," said Timothy diplomatically. "Parisians have called it the 'Ville Lumière' for about two hundred years."

"That's almost the same, isn't it?" said Mrs Renfrew. "How clever the French are!"

Mrs Renfrew did not speak French and took a more generous view of the young man when she discovered that he did. It fell to Timothy's lot to order tickets, arrange cabs, pay bills and act as unofficial courier to the party. He was anxious to be gone from Paris, impatient for the big game to begin. For some reason, he did not anticipate that any harm would come to the girl. This struck him as strange later, but at the moment all his thoughts were centred upon the match between himself and this old French lady who had set herself out to separate him from Mary Maxell.

No unpleasant incident – the crowded condition of the dining-car excepted – marred the journey to Monte Carlo. There was the inevitable night spent in a stuffy sleeping-berth in a car that rocked and swayed to such an extent that Timothy expected it to jump the line, as thousands of other passengers have expected it to do; and they came with the morning to the Valley of the Rhone, a wide, blue, white-flecked stream flowing between gaunt hills, past solitary chateaux and strange walled towns, which looked as if they had been kept under glass cases for centuries, that the modern world should be reminded of the dangers under which our forefathers lived. So to Marseilles, and a long, hot and slow journey to Nice.

To the girl it was a pilgrimage of joy. She would not have missed a single moment of that ride. The blue sea, the white villas with their green jalousies, the banked roses over wall and pergola and the warm-scented breeze, and above all the semi-tropical sun, placed her in a new world, a wonder world more beautiful than imagination had painted.

There is something about Monte Carlo which is very satisfying. It is so orderly, so clean, so white and bright, that you have the impression that it is carefully dusted every morning and that the villas on the hills are taken down weekly by tender hands, polished and replaced.

There is nothing garish about Monte Carlo, for all its stucco and plaster. Some of the buildings, and particularly the Casino, were compared by the irreverent Timothy to the White City, but it was a refined White City and the Casino itself, with its glass-roofed porch, its great, solemn hanging lamps and its decorous uniformed attendants, had something of the air of a National Bank.

Timothy took a room at the Hotel de Paris, where the girl was staying, and lost no time in seeking information.

"Madame Serpilot?" said the concierge. "There is a madame who bears that name, I think, but she is not staying here, monsieur."

"Of whom should I inquire, I pray you?" asked Timothy in the vernacular.

"Of the Municipal Council, monsieur," said the concierge, "or, if the madame is a wealthy madame, of the manager of the Credit Lyonnais, who will perhaps inform monsieur."

"Thanks many times," said Timothy.

He went first to the Credit Lyonnais, and found the manager extremely polite but uncommunicative. It was not the practice of the bank, he said, to disclose the addresses of their clients. He would not say that Madame Serpilot was his client, but if she were, he could certainly not give her address to any unauthorised person. From this Timothy gathered that Madame Serpilot was a client. He went on to the Mairie and met with better fortune. The Mairie had no respect for persons. It was there to supply information and what the Mairie of Monte Carlo does not know about Monaco, the cleverest detective force in the world would be wasting its time trying to discover.

Madame Serpilot lived at the Villa Condamine. The Villa Condamine was not, as the name suggested, in the poorer part of Monte Carlo but in that most exclusive territory, the tiny peninsula of Cap Martin.

"Has madame been a resident long?"

"For one hundred and twenty-nine days," replied the official promptly. "Madame hired the villa furnished from the agent of the

Grand Duchess Eleana who, alas! was destroyed in that terrible revolution."

He gave Timothy some details of the family from which the Grand Duchess had sprung, the amount of her income in pre-war days, and was passing to her eccentricities when Timothy took his departure. He was not interested in the Grand Duchess Eleana, alive or dead.

19

He went to the house agent on the main street and from him procured the exact position of Madame Serpilot's residence.

"An old madame?" said the agent. "No, monsieur, I cannot say that she is old. And I cannot say that she is young."

He thought a moment, as though endeavouring to find some reason for this reticence on the subject of her age, and then added:

"I have not seen her. Madame is a widow," he went on. "Alas! there are so many in France as the result of the terrible war."

"Then she is young," said Timothy. "They didn't send old men to the front."

"She may be young," replied the agent, "or she may be old. One does not know."

He called the assistant who had shown the lady the house and had taken the documents for her to sign. The assistant was aged sixteen, and at the age of sixteen most people above twenty are listed amongst the aged. He was certain she was a widow and very feeble, because she walked with a stick. She always wore a heavy black veil, even when she was in the garden.

"Is it not natural," said the house agent romantically, "that the madame who has lost all that makes life worth living should no longer desire the world to look upon her face?"

"It may be natural in Monte Carlo," said Timothy, "but it is not natural in London."

He located the house on a large plan which the obliging agent produced, and went back to the hotel, firmly resolved to take the first opportunity of calling on Madame Serpilot and discovering what object she had in view when she arranged to endanger his young life.

Mary was waiting for him, a little impatiently for one who had such a horror of gambling.

"We have to get tickets at the Bureau," she said, "and the concierge says we must have special membership cards for the Cercle Privée."

The tickets were easy to procure, and they passed into the great saloon where, around five tables, stood silent ovals of humanity. The scene was a weird one to Timothy and fascinating too. Besides this, all the other gambling games in the world, all the roulette tables and baccara outfits, were crude and amateurish. The eight croupiers who sat at each table in their black frock coats and their black ties, solemn visaged, unemotional, might have been deacons in committee. The click of rakes against chips, the whirr of the twirling ball, the monotonous sing-song annoucement of the chief croupier – it was a ritual and a business at one and the same time.

It was amazing to reflect that, year in and year out, from ten o'clock in the morning until ten o'clock at night (until midnight in the Cercle Privée) these black-coated men sat at their tables, twirling their rakes, watching without error every note or counter that fell on the table, separating notes from chips with a deftness that was amazing, doing this in such an atmosphere of respectability that the most rabid anti-gambler watching the scene must come in time to believe that roulette was a legitimate business exercise.

Through the years this fringe of people about the table would remain, though units would go out, and as units went out new units would replace them, and everlastingly would sit shabby old men and women with their cryptic notebooks, marking their tableaux with red and black pencils, religiously recording the result of every coup, staking now and again their five-franc pieces, and watching them raked to the croupier with stony despair or drawing with trembling hands the few poor francs which fortune had sent them.

Timothy was very silent when they passed the portals of the Cercle Privée, into that wonderful interior which, viewed from the entrance room, had the appearance of some rich cathedral.

"What do you think of them?" asked Mary.

He did not answer at once.

"What did you think of the people?" she demanded again. "Did you see that quaint old woman – taking a chance? I'm sorry," she said quickly, "I really didn't mean to be – "

"I know you didn't," said Timothy, and sighed.

The roulette table did not attract him. He strolled off to watch the players at *trente et quarante*. Here the procedure was more complicated. One of the officials dealt two lines of cards, ending each when the pips added to something over thirty. The top line stood for black, the lower line for red, and that which was nearest to thirty won. After mastering this, the process was simple; you could either back the red or the black, or you could bet that the first card that was dealt was identical with the colour that won, or was the reverse.

The game interested him. It had certain features which in a way were fascinating. He noticed that the croupier never spoke of the black. The black might have had no existence at the *trente et quarante* table; either "red won" or "red lost." He staked a louis and won twice. He staked another and lost it. Then he won three coups of a louis and looked around uncertainly, almost guiltily, for Mary.

She was watching the roulette players, and Timothy took a wad of bills from his pocket and counted out six milles. That was another thing he was to discover: there were three classes of players – those who punted in one or five louis pieces, those who bet handsomely in milles (a thousand franc note is a "mille" and has no other name), and those who went the maximum of twelve thousand francs on each coup.

Money had no value. He threw six thousand down to the croupier and received in exchange six oblong plaques like thin cakes of blue soap. He put a thousand francs on the black and lost it. He looked round apprehensively for Mary, but she was still intent upon the roulette players. He ventured another thousand, and lost that too. A young Englishman sitting at the table looked up with a smile.

"You're betting against the tableau," he said. "The table is running red tonight. Look!"

He showed a little notebook ruled into divisions, and long lines of dots, one under the other. "You see," he said, "all these are reds. The table has only swung across to black twice for any run, and then it was only a run of four. If you bet against the table you'll go broke."

At any other place than at the tables at Monte Carlo advice of this character, and intimate references to financial possibilities, would be resented. But the Rooms, like the grave, level all the players, who are a great family banded together in an unrecognised brotherhood for the destruction of a common enemy.

"I'll take a chance against the table," said Timothy, "and I shall go broke, anyway."

The Englishman laughed.

The four thousand francs he had left went the same way as their friends and Timothy changed another six thousand and threw two on the black. Then, acting on the impulse of the moment, he threw down the remaining four.

"Timothy!"

He turned at the shocked voice and Mary was standing behind him.

"Do you gamble like that?" she asked.

He tried to smile, but produced a grimace.

"Why, it is nothing," he said, "it is only francs, and francs aren't real money, anyway."

She turned and walked away and he followed. The Englishman, twisting round in his chair, said something. Timothy thought he was asking whether he should look after his money and answered "Certainly."

The girl walked to one of the padded benches by the wall and sat down. There was such real trouble in her face that Timothy's heart sank.

"I'm sorry, Mary," he said, "but this is my last fling and you told me I could have it. After tonight I cut out everything that doesn't qualify for the 'earned income' column of the tax surveyor."

"You frighten me," she said. "It isn't the amount of money you were venturing, but there was something in your face which made me feel – why! I just felt sick," she said.

"Mary!" he said in surprise.

"I know I'm being unreasonable," she interrupted, "but Timothy, I – I just don't want to think of you like this."

She looked into his dejected face and the softest light that ever shone in woman's eyes was in hers.

"Poor Timothy!" she said, half in jest, "you're paying the penalty for having a girlfriend."

"I'm paying the penalty for being a loafer," he said huskily. "I think there must be some bad blood in us. Mary, I know what I'm losing," he said, and took one of her hands. "I'm losing the right to love you, dearest."

It was a queer place for such a confession, and in her wildest dreams the girl never imagined that the first word of love spoken to her by any man would come in a gambling saloon at Monte Carlo. Above her where she sat was the great canvas of the Florentine Graces; half nude reliefs on the ceiling dangled glittering chains of light and over all sounded the monotonous voice of the croupier:

"Rouge perd – et couleur."

The young Englishman at the table turned round with an inquiring lift of his eyebrows, and Timothy nodded.

"He wants to know if I'm finished, I suppose," he said, "and honestly Mary, I am. I'm going back to London when this trip's over, and I'm going to start at the bottom and work up."

"Poor Timothy!" she said again.

"I'm not going to lie to you, or pretend any longer. I just love you, Mary, and if you'll wait for me, I'll make good. I have been a gambler," he said, "a poor, low gambler, and all the time I've thought I've been clever! I've been going round puffed up with my own self-importance, and my head's been so much in the air that I haven't seen just where my feet were leading me," he laughed. "This sounds like the sort of thing you get at the Salvation Army penitent form," he said, "but I'm straight and sincere."

"I know you are, Timothy, but you needn't start at the bottom. I have my money – "

"Stop where you are, Mary," he said quietly. "Not a penny would I take from you, darling."

"What did they ring that bell for?" she asked.

It was the second time the tinkle of sound had come from the croupier at the *trente et quarante* table.

"Heaven knows!" said Timothy. "Maybe it is to call the other worshippers."

Again the young Englishman looked round and said something.

"What did he say?" asked Timothy.

"He said seventeen," said the girl. "Was that the number you backed?"

Timothy smiled.

"There are no numbers on that table except No. 1 – and No. 1 is the fat man with the rake – he gets it coming and going. Mary, I'm going to ask you one question: If I make good will you marry me?"

She was silent and again the voice of the croupier came:

"Rouge perd – couleur gagne."

"What does 'rouge perd' mean?" she asked. "He has said that ever so many times."

"It means 'black wins,' " said Timothy.

"Does black always win?" she asked.

"Not always," said Timothy gently. "Maybe he's only saying that to lure me back to the table. Mary, what do you say?"

"I say yes," she said, and to the scandal of the one attendant who was watching them he bent forward and kissed her.

A terrible act this, for the gold-laced and liveried footman, who came with slow, majestic steps to where they sat.

"Monsieur," he said, "this is not done."

Timothy looked up at him.

"*Chassez-vous*," he said firmly.

It was startling French, but it was the nearest he could get at the moment to "chase yourself."

Again the bell tinkled, and the young Englishman rose, thrust a small packet of money into his pocket and came toward them, bearing what looked to be a large book without covers. His face was a little haggard and the perspiration stood upon his forehead.

"This is getting on my nerves, old man. You had better play yourself," he said, and he handed the book to Timothy, and Timothy looked vaguely from his hands to the hot Englishman.

"What's this?" he croaked.

"A run of twenty-eight on the black," said the Englishman. "It is phenomenal! You wanted me to go on, didn't you? I asked you whether I should play your thousand francs. The bank bust four times – didn't you hear them ring for more money?"

Timothy nodded. He had no words.

"Well, your six went to twelve and I left the maximum run," the Englishman said. "I asked you if that was right and you nodded."

"Yes, I nodded," said Timothy mechanically.

"You've won twenty-seven and a half maximums."

Timothy looked at the money in his hand, looked up at the ceiling and gulped something down.

"Thank you," he gasped. "I am obliged to you."

It was inadequate, but it was all that he could say.

"Not at all," said the Englishman. "I won a lot of money myself."

"I'm not a great hand at arithmetic," said Timothy, "will you tell me how many pounds twenty-seven and a half maximums make?"

It was a remarkable situation. Somebody should have laughed, but they were all too serious, the girl as serious as Timothy, and the young Englishman scrawling calculations on a loose page of his notebook.

"Thirty-five francs to a pound," he said, "makes £340 a coup. Twenty-seven and a half is about – "

"Thank you!" said Timothy, and he gripped the other's hand and wrung it. "Thank you, fairy godmother – I don't know your other name."

They stood together watching his lanky figure, as he, wholly unconscious of the providential part he had played, moved down to the roulette table, eyeing the game with the air of superiority which every player of *trente et quarante* has for a game with a paltry maximum of six thousand francs.

"Timothy," whispered the girl, "isn't it wonderful?"

He put the money into his pocket and it bulged untidily.

"What are you going to do with it?" she asked.

"Give it to the poor," said Timothy, taking her arm.

"To the poor?"

She was wondering whether his fortune had driven him mad.

"The poor," he said firmly, "money won by gambling – "

"Nonsense," she broke in, "to what poor are you giving it?"

"To poor Timothy," said he. "Let us dash madly to the bar and drink orangeade."

20

The band was playing one of de Courville's new revue tunes, and the Café de Paris was crowded out. There had been a big influx of visitors from Nice, and Monte Carlo presented an appearance comparable with the height of the season. Mrs Renfrew had motored up to La Turbie, and a bank of cloud having descended upon the mountain made the road dangerous. (Those who have journeyed from the Corniche to Monte Carlo by night will appreciate just how dangerous is that road.) She had, therefore, elected to spend the night at the hotel on the top of the hill.

This information she had telephoned to the girl on the night following Timothy's great win, and had added that she could see "the twinkling lights of Monte Carlo" and that "the misty spaces of ocean filled her with strange unrest," which observation had been repeated to the unsympathetic Timothy.

"It must be awful to have a mind like that," he said, and then, "Mary, I've been a long time waiting to exchange confidences about cousins."

"I have no confidences to give you about Mrs Renfrew," said Mary with a smile, "but you have been on the point of telling me about your cousin so often that I feel a little curious."

The story he had to tell was not a nice one. It meant opening old wounds and reviving sad memories, but it had to be done. She was not so shocked as he had expected.

"You have not told me anything new," she said quietly. "You see, all along I have known that the 'A C' in your name stood for 'Alfred

Cartwright,' and once uncle told me that he had known a relative of yours, and I guessed."

Suddenly she demanded:

"Do you think Cartwright is in Europe?"

Timothy nodded.

"I am certain. That is, if Morocco is in Europe," he said. "I have had it in the back of my mind ever since the crime was committed that that is the place he would make for. You see, in the few minutes I had with him he told me, perhaps not the whole of the story, but at any rate his version. He knows Morocco and has been there before. He spoke about a Moorish chief named El Mograb, who wanted him to stay with the tribe, and he told me he was sorry he had not followed the Moor's advice."

"Did you tell the police that?" she asked.

He shook his head.

"I did not tell the police very much about that visit. Cartwright revived his accusations against Sir John. It meant digging up these charges, and that is what I did not wish to do, for – for – "

"For my sake?" she said quietly.

"That's about the size of it," replied Timothy.

A little stream of diners were leaving the restaurant, moving slowly down the narrow aisle between the tables, and Timothy stopped talking as they passed and eyed them with a bored interest usual to the circumstances.

It was after the interruption had ended, and the last of the little stream had departed, that he saw the card on the table. It was near his place and it had not been there before. He picked it up and on the uppermost side was written: "Do not let your friend see this."

"Well, I'm – " he began, and turned the card over.

It was not written but printed in capital letters:

IF YOU DO NOT HEAR FROM ME BY THE TWENTY-NINTH, I BEG OF YOU THAT YOU WILL GO TO TANGIER AND ENQUIRE AT THE CONTINENTAL HOTEL FOR A MAN CALLED RAHBAT – A MOOR,

WHO WILL LEAD YOU TO ME. I BEG YOU FOR THE SAKE OF OUR RELATIONSHIP TO COME. DID YOU GET THE MONEY?

Timothy laid the card down and stared at the girl.

"What is it?" she asked and reached out her hand.

"I – it is nothing," he said hurriedly.

"Nonsense, Timothy. What is it? Let me see it, please."

Without a word he handed the card to the girl, who read it through in silence.

"Who is that from?" she asked, "Cartwright?"

He nodded.

"Obviously," he said, "the reference to the money and the appeal to our relationship – but how did it get there?"

He called the head waiter.

"Who were those people who went out just now?" he asked.

"They are very well known," explained the head waiter. "There was a monsieur, a London theatrical manager, and a madame who was his wife. There was another monsieur, an American writer, and an English monsieur who was in the employment as secretary to a madame who lives at Cap Martin."

"Madame Serpilot?" asked Timothy quickly.

"Yes, that is the name. She is a widow, *helas!* but immensely rich!"

Timothy put the card into his pocket. He had said nothing to the girl about Madame Serpilot since they had left London, and for the first time he had some misgivings as to her safety. Yet in truth that sixth sense of his, which had hitherto worked so to his advantage, offered him no warning that the girl's happiness was threatened. He was sure that whatever danger the situation held was danger to him personally. He had not seen the English monsieur who was secretary to Madame Serpilot, but then his back had been toward the far end of the room from whence the man came and he had presented no other view than the back of his head.

"It is a message from Cartwright," he said, "and I am going to get to the bottom of this story if I stay in Monte Carlo for the rest of my life."

He saw Mary back to her hotel, went to his room and changed, and just as the Casino was disgorging its tired clients, he walked through the palm-shaded avenue that led to the main road and began his tramp to Cap Martin. To discover a house in this area by daylight, with the aid of a plan, might have been a simple matter – by night it presented almost insuperable difficulties.

Cap Martin is a promontory of hill and pine and wild flowers. Its roads run at the will of its wealthy residents, and there are lanes and paths and broad roads which are not really broad roads at all, but the private entrances to the wonderful villas in which the district abounds, and the grey light was in the eastern sky when Timothy finally located the Villa Condamine.

It stood on the edge of the sea, surrounded on the land side by a high wall, though if its owner sought seclusion the woods which surrounded the villa were sufficient.

Timothy worked round a little bay until be commanded a view of the place from the sea. A zig-zag path led down from the house to the seashore, terminating in a little concrete quay. Presently he heard the sound of footsteps and a Monégasque workman, in blue overalls, came slouching along the shore path, pipe in mouth.

He bade the young man a cheery good morning and stopped, in the friendly way of the Monégasques, to talk. He was a gardener on his way to the villa. He could be on his way to nowhere else, for the rough path on which Timothy stood led straight to a door in the high wall. It was a good job, but he wished he lived nearer. But then, none of madame's servants slept in the house, and –

"Ah! *violà!* It is the Moor!" and he pointed out to sea.

A tiny steam yacht was coming slowly to land – Timothy had seen its lights for an hour – and was steaming now to its anchorage, leaving the line of its wake on the smooth surface of the water.

"The Moor!" said Timothy quickly, and then carelessly, "Has any Moor a villa here?"

"No, monsieur," said the man, "but this is a great Moor who sometimes comes here from Morocco. A long journey, monsieur. It is five days' voyage from the Moorish coast – "

"Does he come to the Villa Condamine?" asked Timothy.

"But yes," said the man. "He is a friend of the madame, and twice has he been there in three months."

There was a little splash of water under the bow of the yacht, when the anchor was dropped, and presently a boat drew away and in the stern sheets was a figure muffled in a white jellab.

Timothy looked after the retreating figure of the gardener, who was leisurely pursuing his way, and, turning, followed him. It was unlikely that the mysterious madame would allow a humble workman to have the key of the garden gate, yet to his surprise this was the case. The man opened the gate and waited, looking round as if he expected somebody. Timothy guessed that there were two or more workmen and that this particular man had the key and admitted the lot. In this surmise he proved to be right. Presently yet another blue-bloused gardener appeared, and the two stood together waiting for a third. He made no appearance, and the two men passed through the door and pulled it close behind them.

Timothy quickened his pace. As he had thought, the door was left ajar for the third man. He pushed it open gently, but saw nothing but the end of a twisting path, which disappeared between high hedges of lilac.

If ever there was a time to take a chance it was now; and he was through the gate, gingerly treading the path, before he realised what he had done. He heard voices and moved with caution. Then, after about five minutes, he heard the garden gate behind him bang. The third workman had arrived and the exit was closed. He made his way through the pines which served to screen the house from observation. There was nobody in sight, and the voices had died away. He could walk more boldly now and came at last to the edge of the wood in full view of the villa. Between him and the house was about fifty yards of clear space. He took a chance and crossed it, his objective being a ground-floor window which was open.

The entrance was not so easily effected as he had expected. The sill of the window was just above the level of his head, and offered no grip to his hands. He made a tour of reconnaissance, but failed to find any other entrance. Behind the sill, he thought, must be a window frame, and stepping back two paces he made a leap and gripped the frame. Quickly he pulled himself up and dropped into the room.

He was conscious of a sweet, fragrant perfume the moment his head became level with the window, and now he saw the explanation. The bare floor was covered three inches thick with rose petals. Evidently the owner made her own perfumery, and this hobby explained the open window. There was no furniture in the room, which was apparently given up to the purpose of drying the petals. The door was unfastened, and he passed into a stone corridor. The structure of the house puzzled him. He did not expect to find himself in the basement; then he remembered that the villa was built on sloping ground, and that the main entrance must be on a higher floor.

A flight of stone steps led to the upper level, and he went up cautiously, a step at a time, and found his exit barred by a door which was fastened on the other side with padlock and staple. It was a primitive method of locking up a cellar, and Timothy, remembering that he had passed a recess filled with garden tools, went back to find the means to remove this obstruction. A long chisel prised the staples from the door with ridiculous ease.

He heard voices speaking in low, guarded tones and moved along the carpeted hall on tiptoe. He listened at the door of the room from which the voices proceeded, and was in two minds as to what his next step should be. The door was one of two let in the same wall. He stopped and brought his ear to the keyhole of the second and there was no sound. Turning the handle, he looked in.

As he expected, it was separated from the other room by a pair of folding doors which were closed. The voices were more distinct but still indistinguishable. He was now in a small drawing-room, well but not luxuriously furnished. Tall French windows led to a loggia, and, what was more important, on either side of these hung long velvet curtains, which might serve, in case of necessity, as a place of concealment.

He heard the door of the next room open, and the voices proceeded along the passage. Then the handle of his own door turned. He had just time to slip behind the curtains before somebody entered. It was a woman, and at the sound of her voice he nearly jumped. She was speaking to somebody in the passage.

"He has gone to his room," she said. "Have your breakfast. He will want you to go into Monte Carlo this morning."

"By daylight?" said the person to whom she spoke, and again Timothy recognised the voice.

"He would not know you with those spectacles. Besides, you had a moustache when you saw him before."

The man in the passage mumbled something, and Timothy heard the door of the room close. There was a desk, he had noticed, against the blank wall of the room, and it was to this she made her way. He heard the scratching of her pen on paper, then he walked from his place of concealment. Her back was to him and she did not hear him until his shadow fell across the table. Then, with a little cry, she leapt up.

"Good morning, Lady Maxell," said Timothy.

21

Sadie Maxell was as white as the paper on which she had been writing.

"How did you get in here?"

Timothy did not answer. He stepped round so that he was between the woman and the door.

"Where is Cartwright?"

"Cartwright?" she repeated. "What do you want to know of him?"

"Lower your voice, if you please," said Timothy sharply. "What is Cartwright to you?"

She licked her dry lips before she spoke. Then:

"I married Cartwright or Benson in Paris – years ago," she said.

Timothy took a step back.

"You married Cartwright," he said incredulously. "That explains why you came away?"

She was looking at him steadily.

"If it wanted any explanation – yes," she said. "What are you going to do?"

"I'm going after the man you have upstairs, the fake Moor, who came into this house half an hour ago, and I'm going to hand him to justice."

Before he knew what had happened, she gripped him by his coat with both hands.

"You are not going to do anything of the kind, Mr 'Take A Chance' Anderson," she said between her teeth, and her voice trembled with passion. "I hated him once, but that was before I knew him. I would sooner see you dead as the other man died than that you should bring him more trouble."

"Let me go," said Timothy, trying to press loose her hands.

"You'll leave this house and forget that you were ever here. Oh, you fool, you fool!"

He had wrenched himself clear of her and flung her backward.

"I have a few words to say to your friend," he said, "and I think you'd better stay here whilst I'm saying them. I hate having family quarrels in public, anyway."

He had not heard the door open behind him and it was the "swish" of the loaded cane which warned him. It did not strike him fair on the head, as was intended, but caught him a glancing blow and he fell on his knees, turning his face to his attacker. He knew it was Brown even before the blow fell.

"Shall I settle him?" said a voice as the stick went up again.

"No, no!" cried the woman, "for God's sake, no!"

It was at that moment that Timothy low-tackled his assailant. Brown tried to strike, but he was too late and went crashing to the floor, his head against the wall. He made one effort to rise, and then with a groan collapsed.

Timothy rose, shaking himself and rubbing his bruised shoulder. Without a word, and with only a look at the woman, he made for the door and banged it in her face. His head was swimming as he made his way up the stairs, swaying at every step. From the broad landing at the top led three doors, only one of which was closed. He turned the handle and went in.

A man was standing by the window, which overlooked the calm expanse of ocean, glittering in the light of the rising sun. From shoulder to heel he was clad in a long white mantle and a dark blue turban encircled his head.

"Now, Cartwright," said Timothy, "you and I will settle accounts."

The man had not moved at the sound of the voice, but when Timothy had finished he turned.

"My God!" cried Timothy. "Sir John Maxell."

CHAPTER THE LAST

"Timothy," said Mary, "I was just thinking about that beautiful house you took me to see at Cap Martin."

"Were you, dear?" said Timothy without any show of interest.

They were on the cross-Channel boat and Boulogne was astern.

"Yes," said the girl. "Do you know, I had a feeling that you had taken me there to show me to somebody, some friend of yours perhaps. All the time I was walking about the garden I had a sense of being watched. It is not an uncomfortable sensation, but just that overlooked feeling one has sometimes. I love Monte Carlo. Do you think we shall go back there after – after – "

"It is likely," said Timothy.

The girl rose and went forward along the deck to get a view of a passing destroyer. Timothy took a letter from his pocket and read it for about the twentieth time. It was undated and began:

My Dear Anderson,

I cannot tell you how grateful I am to you for your kindness and for the big, generous sympathy you have shown me. Especially am I glad that you brought Mary so that I could see her again, for I just hungered for a sight of the child. Won't you please forgive Sadie? She acted without my knowledge but in my interests, as she thought, in trying to keep you away from Monte Carlo after she had planned to bring the girl so that I could see her.

Yes, I killed Cartwright, but I shot him in self-defence. His body lies at the bottom of a disused well in the garden of my house. It is perfectly true that I had been associated in business with him and that I was in his Moorish syndicate and heavily involved. I was so very deeply involved at one time, and so near to ruin that, deceived by some statement which had been made to Sadie's fortune, I made her acquaintance and married her. During the past year I have never ceased to thank God that I did so, for she has been the most loyal companion and friend that a man could desire.

It was I who fired the shot through my own window. I contemplated flight from Cartwright, and was manufacturing evidence against him in advance – God forgive me. Sadie guessed, and when she watched me drawing from the well the bag containing proof that Cartwright's charge was not wholly false, she knew the end was near.

I am perfectly happy, and spend most of my time developing my property in Morocco, under the protection of El Mograb, an old Moorish friend of mine, and the supreme protection of the Sultan, who, as the Pretender, received considerable help from me. I am six months of the year with Sadie, for Sadie either lives on the Riviera or at Cadiz and is easily reachable in my hired yacht.

I think it best for all concerned, and especially for our dear Mary, that I remain as dead. Some day the whole story may be told, but no useful purpose would be served by publishing it today. The card with the message was intended for her, but I am glad that it fell into your hands. As you guessed, it was I who flung Mary's money into your room – I dared not post it to her for fear I was betrayed by my writing, and I knew that you were safe. God bless you both and bring you happiness and prosperity, to which I hope this property of mine will one day contribute.

Timothy folded the letter and was putting it in his pocket, then changed his mind and took it out. He read it again, then tore it into pieces and flung it over the side of the ship.

Then he too went forward to the wife he had married in Paris – much against the wishes of a scandalised Mrs Renfrew – who nevertheless termed it "a pretty romance" in the article she wrote for the *Bath County Herald*.

EDGAR WALLACE

BIG FOOT

Footprints and a dead woman bring together Superintendent Minton and the amateur sleuth Mr Cardew. Who is the man in the shrubbery? Who is the singer of the haunting Moorish tune? Why is Hannah Shaw so determined to go to Pawsy, 'a dog lonely place' she had previously detested? Death lurks in the dark and someone must solve the mystery before BIG FOOT strikes again, in a yet more fiendish manner.

BONES IN LONDON

The new Managing Director of Schemes Ltd has an elegant London office and a theatrically dressed assistant – however Bones, as he is better known, is bored. Luckily there is a slump in the shipping market and it is not long before Joe and Fred Pole pay Bones a visit. They are totally unprepared for Bones' unnerving style of doing business, unprepared for his unique style of innocent and endearing mischief.

Edgar Wallace

Bones of the River

'Taking the little paper from the pigeon's leg, Hamilton saw it was from Sanders and marked URGENT. *Send Bones instantly to Lujamalababa… Arrest and bring to head-quarters the witch doctor.*'

It is a time when the world's most powerful nations are vying for colonial honour, a time of trading steamers and tribal chiefs. In the mysterious African territories administered by Commissioner Sanders, Bones persistently manages to create his own unique style of innocent and endearing mischief.

The Daffodil Mystery

When Mr Thomas Lyne, poet, poseur and owner of Lyne's Emporium insults a cashier, Odette Rider, she resigns. Having summoned detective Jack Tarling to investigate another employee, Mr Milburgh, Lyne now changes his plans. Tarling and his Chinese companion refuse to become involved. They pay a visit to Odette's flat. In the hall Tarling meets Sam, convicted felon and protégé of Lyne. Next morning Tarling discovers a body. The hands are crossed on the breast, adorned with a handful of daffodils.

EDGAR WALLACE

THE JOKER

While the millionaire Stratford Harlow is in Princetown, not only does he meet with his lawyer Mr Ellenbury but he gets his first glimpse of the beautiful Aileen Rivers, niece of the actor and convicted felon Arthur Ingle. When Aileen is involved in a car accident on the Thames Embankment, the driver is James Carlton of Scotland Yard. Later that evening Carlton gets a call. It is Aileen. She needs help.

THE SQUARE EMERALD

'Suicide on the left,' says Chief Inspector Coldwell pleasantly, as he and Leslie Maughan stride along the Thames Embankment during a brutally cold night. A gaunt figure is sprawled across the parapet. But Coldwell soon discovers that Peter Dawlish, fresh out of prison for forgery, is not considering suicide but murder. Coldwell suspects Druze as the intended victim. Maughan disagrees. If Druze dies, she says, 'It will be because he does not love children!'

OTHER TITLES BY EDGAR WALLACE AVAILABLE DIRECT FROM HOUSE OF STRATUS

Quantity		£	$(US)	$(CAN)	€
☐	THE FOURTH PLAGUE	6.99	11.50	15.99	11.50
☐	THE FRIGHTENED LADY	6.99	11.50	15.99	11.50
☐	GOOD EVANS	6.99	11.50	15.99	11.50
☐	THE HAND OF POWER	6.99	11.50	15.99	11.50
☐	THE IRON GRIP	6.99	11.50	15.99	11.50
☐	THE JOKER	6.99	11.50	15.99	11.50
☐	THE JUST MEN OF CORDOVA	6.99	11.50	15.99	11.50
☐	THE KEEPERS OF THE KING'S PEACE	6.99	11.50	15.99	11.50
☐	THE LAW OF THE FOUR JUST MEN	6.99	11.50	15.99	11.50
☐	THE LONE HOUSE MYSTERY	6.99	11.50	15.99	11.50
☐	THE MAN WHO BOUGHT LONDON	6.99	11.50	15.99	11.50
☐	THE MAN WHO KNEW	6.99	11.50	15.99	11.50
☐	THE MAN WHO WAS NOBODY	6.99	11.50	15.99	11.50
☐	THE MIND OF MR J G REEDER	6.99	11.50	15.99	11.50
☐	MORE EDUCATED EVANS	6.99	11.50	15.99	11.50
☐	MR J G REEDER RETURNS	6.99	11.50	15.99	11.50
☐	RED ACES	6.99	11.50	15.99	11.50
☐	ROOM 13	6.99	11.50	15.99	11.50
☐	SANDERS	6.99	11.50	15.99	11.50
☐	SANDERS OF THE RIVER	6.99	11.50	15.99	11.50
☐	THE SINISTER MAN	6.99	11.50	15.99	11.50
☐	THE SQUARE EMERALD	6.99	11.50	15.99	11.50
☐	THE THREE JUST MEN	6.99	11.50	15.99	11.50
☐	THE THREE OAK MYSTERY	6.99	11.50	15.99	11.50
☐	THE TRAITOR'S GATE	6.99	11.50	15.99	11.50
☐	WHEN THE GANGS CAME TO LONDON	6.99	11.50	15.99	11.50
☐	WHEN THE WORLD STOPPED	6.99	11.50	15.99	11.50

Hotline: UK ONLY: **0800 169 1780,** please quote author, title and credit card details.
INTERNATIONAL: **+44 (0) 20 7494 6400,** please quote author, title and credit card details.

Send to: **House of Stratus Sales Department**
24c Old Burlington Street
London
W1X 1RL
UK

Please allow for postage costs charged per order plus an amount per book as set out in the tables below:

	£(Sterling)	$(US)	$(CAN)	€(Euros)
Cost per order				
UK	2.00	3.00	4.50	3.30
Europe	3.00	4.50	6.75	5.00
North America	3.00	4.50	6.75	5.00
Rest of World	3.00	4.50	6.75	5.00
Additional cost per book				
UK	0.50	0.75	1.15	0.85
Europe	1.00	1.50	2.30	1.70
North America	2.00	3.00	4.60	3.40
Rest of World	2.50	3.75	5.75	4.25

PLEASE SEND CHEQUE, POSTAL ORDER (STERLING ONLY), EUROCHEQUE, OR INTERNATIONAL MONEY ORDER (PLEASE CIRCLE METHOD OF PAYMENT YOU WISH TO USE)
MAKE PAYABLE TO: STRATUS HOLDINGS plc

Cost of book(s): ________ Example: 3 x books at £6.99 each: £20.97
Cost of order: ________ Example: £2.00 (Delivery to UK address)
Additional cost per book: ________ Example: 3 x £0.50: £1.50
Order total including postage: ________ Example: £24.47

Please tick currency you wish to use and add total amount of order:

☐ £ (Sterling) ☐ $ (US) ☐ $ (CAN) ☐ € (EUROS)

VISA, MASTERCARD, SWITCH, AMEX, SOLO, JCB:

☐☐☐☐☐☐☐☐☐☐☐☐☐☐☐☐☐☐☐☐

Issue number (Switch only):

☐☐☐

Start Date: ☐☐/☐☐ **Expiry Date:** ☐☐/☐☐

Signature: ________

NAME: ________

ADDRESS: ________

____

POSTCODE: ________

Please allow 28 days for delivery.

Prices subject to change without notice.
Please tick box if you do not wish to receive any additional information. ☐

House of Stratus publishes many other titles in this genre; please check our website (**www.houseofstratus.com**) for more details.